FRATS

BASED ON TRUE EVENTS

DEE SNIDER

FRATS

Published by Red Penguin Books

Bellerose Village, New York

ISBN

Print 978-1-63777-389-5 / 978-1-63777-390-1

Digital 978-1-63777-388-8

CONTENTS

At this point, my Dee-hard followers (and I thank you for your dedication to my various artistic endeavors) may be starting to think I sound like a broken record. On virtually everything I've ever done, I've dedicated it to my wife and partner in life, Suzette. The fact is without her support and undying love (not to mention her belief in me), I would never have achieved and done all the things I have. Besides artistically helping and inspiring me creatively, she has always "held down the fort" with our family and home, allowing me to create and explore my creativity.

So, Suzette, this book is dedicated to you. Thank you for everything you have done and continue to do that allows me to do the things I love to do. I love you…forever.

(Those of you in the know may notice some similarities between the courtship of the fictional couple in this book and my own real-life one with Suzette. Hey, you gotta go with what you know!)

CHAPTER ONE

February 1999, Long Island, New York.

The morning rush.

This is my carpool's daily grind. Back and forth from the suburbs to the city, five days a week—virtually every week of the year—year after year, with a few days off for holidays, vacations, and misadventures. Nothing worse than a wasted day off caused by some bug the kids brought home or from an embarrassing injury.

"I didn't fall; my rollerblades got caught on a crack in the bike path."

Humbling.

And no commute was more brutal than the one from the suburbs of Suffolk County to midtown Manhattan. The Long Island roadway system was a congested, ill-conceived joke.

The east/west running Northern State Parkway, built in 1933 by urban planner Robert Moses, included an unnatural dip in the road that took commuters two miles due south. Put in place to assuage a group of wealthy, North Shore landowners, for a mere $175,000 donation to the Long Island State Park Commission (and at an additional cost of

$2.75 million for the execution of the diversion), ol' Bob Moses routed the NSP around their posh Old Westbury estates instead of going through them. Even though their massive properties have long since been sold off and subdivided, that backroom deal added an average of an hour onto the daily trip to and from work, ultimately stealing more than a year of life from the everyday commuter over the course of his or her working career. So for myself and my other fellow forty-something voyagers—except for James, who at 28 had barely begun his life journey—we've still got a lot of living to lose.

And today it was raining.

It was my day to drive, so I couldn't even catch a little shuteye like the others. I just sat there behind the wheel, barely inching along, serenaded by a low-volume news radio station playing in the background and the hypnotic sound of the windshield wipers doing their job.

Schwump – schwump – schwump – schwump.

At least they weren't squeaking.

Long ago I had that life-affirming moment that puts everything into perspective and made even a bad day okay. It could be worse…it could be raining. Not the best catchphrase to reference considering that it was…but you get my drift. I learned to let the small stuff go…life was way too short.

This said, I couldn't help but notice how faceless we all were. Just five corporate drones, riding in another four-door sedan, in an iceberg-slow sea of black, grey, brown, silver, and white. All blending perfectly with our dreary surroundings on a late winter's day; so drab and devoid of color the world appears sepia.

Why didn't I buy the red car? I really wanted the re–

Suddenly, the idiot in front of me stopped short, forcing me to jam on the brakes and narrowly avoiding a collision that would have made this terrible morning a lot worse.

Well, that woke up my fellow weary travelers.

I slammed the horn, using the surrogate to blare my anger at the offending vehicle in front of me.

The driver of the now fully-stopped car rolled down his window, stuck his arm out into the rain, and flicked me the international symbol of defiance for the ages: "The Bird."

I started to roll down my window to respond with the obligatory, "Asshole!" when something caught my eye. The license plate on the guy's car had only three letters: D G N…

"Follow me!" Brett yelled and, using his good arm, pulled me toward the house we were standing in front of.

"Where the hell are we going?!" I said, falling in behind him. "Do you know the people who live here!?"

"This way!" Brett commanded.

With the pack of Delta Gamma Nu members close behind, we headed into the backyard and literally ran for our lives.

The gang desperately tried to follow, but not knowing the lay of the land like Brett, they were stumbling, bumbling, and fumbling the entire way. As we climbed over fence after fence, running from yard to yard, they even mixed it up with a few dogs who, already agitated from not sinking their teeth into Brett and me, were extra aggressive when one of the Gamma Nu assholes leaped over. Woof.

By the time we exited the last yard on the block, we were on a cross street with a big lead.

"Come on!" Brett barked, and I followed.

We went back across Forest Avenue, then dove into the yards of houses fronting on Centennial Avenue. When we finally got to the dry stream-bed behind Brookside Avenue, we quickly tucked ourselves under the Centennial Avenue overpass and hid. Brett and I waited, breathing heavily, not saying a word, and listening for any sign of Delta Gamma Nu…

"Delta Gamma Nu," I said absentmindedly. I hadn't thought of them in years.

"What's that, Robert?" asked Marie, sitting next to me, as she checked her makeup in the passenger visor mirror.

"The letters on that car's license plate—DGN. They stand for Delta Gamma Nu."

"What's that, a college fraternity?" asked James, desperately trying to adjust his long legs for a bit more comfort as it was his turn to get stuck behind me this morning...and I'm not a little guy.

"A *high school* fraternity," I clarified.

"They don't have fraternities in high school...do they?" Tommy chimed in from the sweet seat behind petite Marie.

"I didn't think they did either until my family moved to the south shore of Nassau County. There were a ton of them in the '70s."

"So what were they, like a high school version of a college fraternity thing?" Alex asked, riding the hump in the netherworld of the middle back seat stuck between comfortable and cramped. "I pledged Gamma Lambda Phi in college."

"They started out that way," I replied. "The first one was founded in the late '30s at a high school in Brooklyn—Beta Lambda Rho—Blue and Gold were their colors. Only the elite young men of the school were allowed to join. You had to be one of the best students, best athletes, and best citizens to be asked to pledge BLR. Oh yeah...*and a white Christian.*"

"Is that true?" Marie demanded, indignant, as she was neither.

I had all of my associates' full attention now.

"Sure was, but not for long. Over the next couple of decades all kinds of high school "frats" were created for pretty much every clique, but they soon turned into nothing more than glorified gangs. They practically ruled several towns on the South Shore...until they were finally banned in the early '80s for being too violent."

"How do you know so much about them?" Tom asked.

"I was in one for a while."

This last statement seemed to satisfy any further interest the riders had on the subject, each going back to their own private thoughts and reveries…but not me.

The conversation brought back more memories I had worked hard to forget. I couldn't stop thinking about that dark period in my life. Maybe that was why my hand reached up to the hair covering my forehead and unconsciously brushed it away exposing a massive ugly scar.

Marie noticed immediately.

"Oh my God, Robert! What happened to your head!?"

Her horror got the attention of the fading trio in the back who leaned over to get a closer look.

"Holy shit, Kovac! That scar is nasty!" James exclaimed.

"It looks like the top of your head got torn off!" Alex practically shouted. "How the hell did you get that!?"

For a moment, I considered keeping my terrible secret a little longer, but as I looked around at the crawling traffic and the New York City skyline still barely visible in the distance, I decided to tell the truth I'd always wanted to tell—no, the truth I needed to tell. Besides, it was Y2K…this could be my last chance. The story had become a fast-fading memory that sometimes seemed more like a bad dream. But we should never forget our darkest, most life-changing secrets. Those awful memories keep us from letting them happen again.

"Well," I began, "I grew up on Wright-Patterson Air Force base in Dayton, Ohio."

"You were an Air Force brat?" Marie asks.

"It was a lot more normal than it sounds," I say semi-defensively. "We had a pretty typical house, and my kid sister and I went to a normal school and hung out with friends—all that regular stuff—while my dad worked nine to five doing aircraft R&D."

"R&D?" Alex asked.

"Research and Development," I clarified.

"So, what kind of kid were you?" James probed

"At Wright-Patterson?" I answered. "Typical I guess, honor roll, good in sports, pretty popular."

"Oh yeah, real typical," Tom replied snarkily.

"You forgot handsome and class president," Marie added with a laugh.

"I was never class president," I said seriously. "But I was vice president."

Now everybody laughed; I did, too.

"But that all changed with 'The Move'," I added, suddenly somber. "I had no idea I was heading into a nightmare that would completely change who I was...and almost kill me."

That comment and the huge keloid scar on my head quickly sobered up my passengers. As I started the story they asked me to tell, I instinctively pulled my hair back over my scar.

CHAPTER TWO

In 1972, my father was offered a great job opportunity in the civilian sector at Grumman Aerospace in Bethpage, Long Island, so the family closed up shop in Dayton and headed east. No one ever asked me if I wanted to move; back then you didn't consult your kids on something significant like that. Today? Today there would be a family meeting and a vote before any new employment would even be considered and any move made. I'm not sure if that's better or worse. But this job was a step up for my family economically and away from the military for my dad, so it was a done deal; no questions asked.

And forget about the other life-changing aspects of the move: where and when? My father picked the date we would leave and the town and the house where we would be living. I don't even think my mother had a say in it. My dad found a place he thought was suitable for the family, the movers were called, and on August 4th we moved into 33 Ardmore Road, Baldwin, Long Island. It was the summer of Watergate and the Vietnam Conflict with all the protests going on—important stuff—but I was going to be a high school senior. All I could think about was how I'd fit in at my new school.

I remember turning onto our block for the first time after a 10-hour, two-day drive from Dayton thinking, *What kind of name is Ardmore?* Then I saw a kid—no more than 12—with no hair; bald. A little farther down there was a young man with severe cerebral palsy being helped into a car, and I joked to myself, *Oh, it's Odd-more Road.* I know that's not a nice thing to say, but it was the '70s, and I was a stupid teenager. It's not an excuse, but back then people thought and said insensitive things like that all the time. Anyway, it wouldn't be too long before I would become an addition to the curiosities on my block.

Pulling up at our new house, I was suddenly overloaded with information. As my dad promised, it was a step up from where we lived at Wright-Patterson; but as I looked around, I was taken aback by how similar our new house looked to the one next door and across the street: two stories, attached one-car garage, small porch, picture window, decorative faux shutters on the windows, and two trees. This was the post-war suburban sprawl that I had heard about...and now I was living in it.

The massive moving truck was already there, and a squad of matching jumpsuit-wearing movers was already unloading our life. That's right; movers used to wear matching uniforms with their names on them. My dad had barely stopped the car before my mother jumped out running and started barking orders at the annoyed movers. Just like a military wife. Shaking his head, my dad got out of the car and joined the fray, leaving my sister and me sitting in the back seat in shock. Suzy may have been only 11, but she was as devastated by what was happening as I was. We just sat there numb for almost five minutes watching the insanity and looking around at our new neighbors. Some stood in a group across the street openly pointing and assessing the kind of people we were by our furniture and the year, make, and model of our car. Ours was a recently purchased Buick Le Sabre complete with a yellowing window sticker showing all the options and the price my dad paid for the vehicle; a thankfully long-gone way of displaying social status. Other less obvious neighbors watched from the safety of their front porches. Some simply stared out of their picture window at "the new people."

Eventually, Suzy and I got out of the car—mainly because with the car turned off and the windows rolled up, the interior had turned into an inferno in the August heat and humidity—and ventured cautiously toward the house. Being six years older than my sister, we never really had much in common; but at that moment, as we walked through that front door, we were never closer.

There were already some pieces of furniture, still covered with blankets, boxes, and packing materials, dropped haphazardly in the rooms the movers thought they were supposed to be in, but there was nothing that made either of us feel like we belonged. We climbed the stairs to what would be our bedrooms on the second floor. There were two identical dormer rooms on either side of the staircase with a little bathroom dead in the center; our feeling of disorientation grew.

"Which room is mine, Bobby?" Suzy asked, confused.

"There's a difference?" I answered, knowing full well that there really wasn't. "I don't know, which do you want, the front or the back?"

"I guess I'll take the front. I want to see what's going on," she said.

"That's perfect because I don't."

I know it sounds like I was a spoiled teen, but being suddenly uprooted after spending your entire life in one place can really rock your world. I think I was understandably upset.

Just then, two movers plowed blindly up the stairs, each carrying a stack of boxes, and nearly bowled us over.

"Out of the way, kids," one of the talking boxes barked, and Suzy and I squeezed into the glorified shoebox of a bathroom.

"I gotta get out of here," I said more to myself than Suzy.

"Where are you going?"

"Back to Dayton," I replied only half-kidding.

As I exited the house into the smothering heat and humidity of a Long Island mid-summer day, I passed my mother and father who were fighting the good fight: Man vs. Movers. Man never wins.

"Where do you think you're going?" It was more of a statement than a question. What he was really saying was, "You're not going anywhere."

"There's nothing for me to do here, Dad. I'm just in the way."

"Nothing to do? We're moving into a new house, for Chrissakes! There's nothing but things to–"

"Senior?" my mom interrupted.

That's right; I'm Robert Kovac, Junior. Keep it to yourself, and if anybody calls me Junior...*I'll kill you.*

My dad looked at my mom with a degree of incredulity. Being a sergeant major in the Air Force, there were not many people who could question his orders...but that never stopped my mom. Still, he didn't like it.

"They're just moving everything into the house. There really isn't much Bobby can do until they're done," she finished.

"So where are you going?" my dad felt safe asking.

"I'm gonna check out the neighborhood. See what's around."

"Well, be back by six, and we'll all go out for some Chinese food," my mom said.

In the early '70s going out for dinner wasn't a common thing; most meals were cooked and eaten at home. "Going out for Chinese" was kind of a big deal, usually reserved for special occasions...like destroying my life.

As I headed down the driveway toward my destiny, my mother shouted...

"Maybe you'll make a new friend!"

* * *

I was so miserable, the thought was inconceivable. I knew I was going to die alone in Baldwin, Long Island. And I almost did.

If I thought the feeling of disorientation was strong at our new house, it was even stronger as I ventured into the completely uncharted territory of my new neighborhood. Alien surroundings. During the summer, the normal social rhythm of any community was completely disrupted. Vacations, summer and day camp, families visiting, visiting families, and even a backyard pool could completely change the dynamics of a neighborhood. I remember one quiet, lonely kid in Dayton who had the only pool in the area, and his house was literally the center of civilization all summer long. From Memorial Day to Labor Day, everybody was his best friend. But once summer was over, nobody wanted to know him; he was unpopular again. Totally screwed up, I know, but true. The point is, you really can't judge a neighborhood by the summer activity, or lack thereof...but I did. I hadn't gotten more than a few houses down the block and was already filled with hopelessness and desperation. My senior year of high school was ruined.

"Hey!"

My train of thought was instantly derailed as I turned to the voice. Sitting on the front steps of a house was a short, thin, average-looking kid with "car doors" for ears. My guess was he was a junior or a senior in high school.

"You the new kid?" he asked rhetorically. Who else would I be?

I winced at the designation, knowing I would be the new kid for quite a while, or at least until some newer new kid moved to town.

"Regrettably," I replied, noticing that "car doors" was holding a comic book with a small stack of others by his side.

"Good answer. My name's Brett Pearson."

"Bobby Kovac. What are you reading?"

"The premier issue of *Defenders* with Hulk, Dr. Strange and–"

"Submariner. Yeah, I know. What else you got?" I asked, crossing the front lawn and joining him on the stoop.

Brett was practically beside himself.

"Issue #5 of *Ghost Rider*—he is so cool—and the latest Marvel Team-up with Spiderman and the Human Torch…"

We were off to the races.

Back then, comic books were pretty dorky, but I loved them. They were something I discovered the year my dad banned television in our house. He said it was to get back to having conversations, reading books, making models, and playing board games, but I'm pretty sure it was because our TV broke and he didn't want to spend the money to buy a new one. Thankfully, that Spartan edict only lasted for several months, but it was long enough to get me hooked on superheroes, which may have had something to do with what led me down my dangerous path…but I'm getting ahead of myself.

Brett wasn't the type I usually hung around with. In Dayton, I played a lot of sports, so most of my friends had been jock types. Brett was anything but an athlete, but he had a great sense of humor, and besides comic books, we liked a lot of the same music, hard rocking stuff like Deep Purple, Led Zeppelin, and Black Sabbath. For the entire month of August, Brett and I became constant companions, hanging out together pretty much every day. And I was glad to have him.

Not yet being able to drive, our world was limited to the immediate neighborhood and whatever might be within walking distance from our block. Sure, we could have ridden our bicycles, but I was a soon-to-be high school senior with my driver's test on the horizon. As an image-conscious teen, I didn't think it was cool for me to be seen riding a bicycle. Ridiculous I know, but for some reason, I just didn't want that to be my first impression as the new kid. Brett still rode his bike, but out of respect for my absurd image concerns, he didn't ride it whenever he was with me.

Now, when you're an adult, towns are pretty much a series of pass-throughs. You pass through one part to get to where you live, through another to go to the local shops. Kind of what John Lennon said about life, "It's what happens to you while you're busy making other plans." A town is what you pass through when you're going other places.

Brett had lived in Baldwin his whole life. Nobody knows the ins and outs of their town like a kid who has spent his entire existence in one place, incrementally coming to know every square inch as they grow up and their parent's slowly let out their leash. I knew my neighborhood in Dayton like a trained rat knows his maze. But I wasn't in Dayton anymore. When you're young, you have both the time and inclination to study the minutiae of your surroundings. No child goes through life with their head up, facing forward, fully fixated on their next destination as adults do. There is nothing around a young kid that isn't worth their full attention. Brett had learned his North Baldwin topography like an expert cartographer.

During those four hot, humid weeks in August, Brett was my tour guide to every street, path, alleyway, nook, and cranny in reasonable—and not so reasonable—walking distance of where we lived.

"Wait'll you see this!" — "You gotta see this!" — "You won't believe this!" he'd say.

Sometimes his enthusiasm didn't match the things he was showing me...but other times it did.

Like every other community, there were stories—both real and urban legend, the sublime to the ridiculous—to go with each location. And virtually all of the stories were dark or shady involving injury, intrigue, or even murder: "And all that they found left of Mrs. Johnson's body was a piece of her ear!"

Nobody wants to hear the boring truth: "Mrs. Johnson walked out on her husband, and all she left behind was an earring."

Give me the urban legend any day.

In our small corner of Baldwin, there was a park (Coes Neck), a field (Clyde), about an acre of treed overgrown land (The Woods), and a sledding hill (Suicide). Suicide Hill was a perfect example of reality turned into urban legend. The mildly steep hill was directly next to a large cement sewer pipe and was originally called Sewer Side Hill. Get it? Over the years 'Sewer Side' got slurred into 'Suicide' which eventually evolved into a true story about a local sledder—whose name for some reason not a single kid in the neighborhood could remember— who on a particularly fast run, lost control, crashed into the cement sewer pipe, "split his head right open," and died; hence Suicide Hill. That's a much better name and story.

Now, my favorite North Baldwin local kid secret was a dry creek bed that wound itself for miles behind dozens and dozens of homes and buildings. The only time this thing ever had water in it was after a tumultuous rainstorm, and the runoff from the sewer grates on the streets that spilled directly into it would fill it up. This was probably the sole purpose of "The Brook" (as it was known), yet as much of a non-brook as this glorified aqueduct was, there were still homeowners who literally built bridges across it and docks that abutted it for their "life on the waterfront." Go figure.

It was things like that dry creek bed that no adult—other than the ones who lived on it—would even know existed, but there wasn't a kid in the neighborhood who hadn't explored its length and vast mysteries. Last I heard, Clyde Field and The Woods had been turned into a condo development (probably called "Clyde Condominiums" or "Suicide Suites") and The Brook has been lined with cement for better flow of rain runoff. It's kind of sad really.

That summer of '72 was the last time I would have any connection with the child I once was. I fondly remember hanging with Brett, and we got really close; but sadly, my childhood was over the day I walked into Baldwin Senior High School. And before too long, so was my friendship with Brett.

CHAPTER THREE

W alking through the doors of the school that first day wasn't too bad. The shortest way in from where we lived was through the back entrance, so the initial Brett Pearson Tour was pretty straightforward. As we made our way down the crowded hallway, he gave me the play-by-play.

"Here's where our lockers will be. No need to stop unless you want to practice putting in and taking out imaginary books?"

"No, I'm good," I said absently.

"That's the west wing stairway to the second floor," Brett continued. "If anybody offers to sell you an elevator pass, don't buy it."

"Why not?" I said, thinking that an elevator pass might be a cool thing to have.

" 'Cause there's no elevator in this school," Brett answered flatly.

"Good to know."

"In case you can't read, that's the dean's office," Brett said, pointing to a door clearly marked "Ethel Kloberg, Dean of Students."

Strange name.

"And this is the cafeteria," Brett continued. "Me and my friends sit over at that table in the corner."

"Cool," I said, not exactly sure why.

As we passed through the halls, it felt like pretty much everyone was sizing me up. I was starting to feel a bit like a bug under a microscope, but to be fair, I was checking them out, too. Where the hell was I going to fit in?

"And through these doors…" Brett announced dramatically.

We entered a cavernous lobby area filled with students standing, sitting, talking, yelling, coming in, and heading out. The high ceilings, terrazzo floors, and floor-to-ceiling plate glass windows amplified and echoed every sound.

"This is 'The Commons'!" he finished with a flourish. You would have thought he had conjured it up.

I was instantly overwhelmed by this melting pot of high school humanity as Brett continued his diatribe, pointing as he spoke like he was directing traffic.

"Against that window are the Jocks. Directly next to them are the Freaks and Hippies. Over against that wall are all the Smart Kids; you know, the ones in the advanced classes. Next to them are the choir, band, and theater geeks. And directly across from the Jocks against that wall by the gym is where the dirtbags and troublemakers sit...when they're not cutting class and hanging out on the side of Woolworths. The rest of the walls are filled with various other lesser groups and cliques."

"So where do you and your friends sit?" I asked, my head spinning with new information.

"Nowhere," replied Brett matter-of-factly. "Me and my friends don't fit in with any group." Then he added as a caveat, "But we have our table in the lunch room! You can sit with us."

Any port in a storm, I thought to myself.

From behind us, I heard a coquettish voice, "Hey, Brent Peterson, who's your friend."

We both turned to see a hot blond with two equally hot friends approaching. Each was wearing a distinctive two-colored sweater with Greek letters, and all three had me under a microscope as Brett responded, more than a little surprised.

"Oh, hi, Cindy" Brett answered, not even considering correcting her on his name. "This is Bobby Kovac; he's new.

"I like that," Cindy said suggestively. "Well, Bobby Kovac, this is Aimee and Joanne; we're Theta girls. You need to pledge Delta."

With that, the three turned and strutted off, leaving Brett in shock and me confused by our brief exchange.

"She has never spoken to me before," Brett said in disbelief. "I can't believe she almost knew my name."

"So, what's a Theta girl?" I asked, my curiosity piqued. "And what the hell does 'pledge Delta' mean?"

"Seriously? You haven't noticed?" Brett said, answering my questions with questions. "Look around you, Bobby; they're everywhere." He gestured to the entire Commons area. "The frats."

I looked around, truly focusing for the first time as Brett went down the list.

"Against those windows—the Jocks. The ones in the Blue and Gold jackets, T-shirts, and sweaters are Beta Lambda Rho. They're one of the biggest fraternities; elite white Christians only. That's their "sister sorority," Alpha Pi Epsilon, sitting with them in the red and white; mostly cheerleaders and the hottest white, Christian chicks."

"Right next to them," Brett continued, "are the other big dogs at Baldwin High, Delta Zeta Theta, Black and Green. They're the ones Cindy said you should pledge for. They're also an elite, jocks-only fraternity, but they don't discriminate. In fact, one of the only black kids in our school is a member. Their sister sorority is Theta Tau Mu —Purple and Blue—Theta girls."

Cindy, who was now sitting with her other sorority sisters and the DZO fraternity members, noticed Brett and me looking over at them and blew me a kiss. Brett was on a roll and didn't take notice of this silent exchange as he plowed on with his Baldwin High School fraternity master class.

"Now directly across from Delta and Beta sits Black and Grey. Then there's Tau Zeta Epsilon—Red and White, Beta Kappa Phi—Black and Blue, and Black and Purple—Kappa Mu Theta. Black and Grey is for athletes who couldn't get into the other jock frats, TZE is a Jews-only frat, and remember those dirtbags and troublemakers I pointed out before? Well, Black and Blue and Black and Purple are the frats most of them belong to. They are not nice guys. Each of the fraternities has a standing membership ranging from 15 to 50 plus, with other "chapters" in neighboring towns."

"And this is okay with the school?" I asked. I couldn't believe they were allowed to parade around wearing their "colors." Though I did have to admit, they looked pretty cool.

"Sure," Brett said. "They have charters registered with the police and everything."

"So is that all?" I asked sarcastically, trying to take in everything Brett was sharing.

"Pretty much," responded Brett. "Oh, there are a handful of other smaller frats with lesser memberships, like Delta Omega Gamma, for example. Their colors are Green and White."

Delta Omega Gamma. I quickly ran the acronym for the frat's name. D-O-G...*dog*? Guess their founding members didn't think that one through. And their green and white jackets made them look like fans of the New York Jets.

"WHAT THE FUCK ARE YOU LOOKIN' AT!?"

A loud, booming voice cut through the Commons, stopping every conversation and action within earshot. The potential for conflict was clearly implied by the hostile tone of the question.

Brett and I turned and saw a large, black-and-green, frat-jacket-wearing Neanderthal striding toward us. The last thing I wanted on my first day of school was a fight, especially with this angry gorilla. Brett literally seemed to shrivel up in anticipation of the coming confrontation. He would be no help. But before I could make any kind of move to avoid trouble, trouble was in my face.

"I SAID, WHAT THE FUCK ARE YOU LOOKIN' AT?!"

As the "fight or flight" neurons fired in my brain, completely unexpectedly, Brett stepped in between us.

"Heh-hey, Big John; he's new here. He didn't know any bett–"

Big John's arm shot out and grabbed Brett by the throat like a cobra.

"I know he's the new kid, Piss-on," the moron cleverly growled at Brett Pearson. "But if you want some of my attention, too–"

This was Big John "One Punch" Russo, a perfect caricature of a high school bully, and as I found out later, Cindy's boyfriend. He wasn't too happy with the attention she had shown me.

"Let him go," I heard myself say. I couldn't help it. I didn't want to fight, but I couldn't let him take his hostility toward me out on Brett. Especially after the little guy had kinda-sorta stood up for me.

"Okay," Big John hissed. "I'll let him go, Cunt-vacs."

This cretin was a laugh riot.

Then he turned and threw a wide haymaker at my head, which I easily sidestepped, causing him to fall forward past me.

There were a few cautious snickers from onlookers, which sent ol' One Punch into a fury.

"AHHHHH!" he roared as he charged at me swinging.

I easily dodged his punch again, and he thundered past me, coming up empty once more. As it turned out, the One Punch nickname wasn't given to him for how quickly he took out an opponent, but rather that he had once been knocked out with one punch. Nicknames are rarely given as compliments. I knew a guy whose nickname was "Ramrod" and trust me, it wasn't because he had a big one. Friends can be cruel.

By now people, including Big John's fraternity brothers, were openly laughing.

"All right, enough," said a controlling voice.

It belonged to another Delta member; the voice approached me with Theta girl Joanne close behind.

"At ease, One Punch," he commanded Big John with more than a hint of sarcasm. "I got this."

Big John was red in the face with anger and embarrassment, but he did as he was told.

"I'm Billy Russell, captain of the varsity football team and president of the Baldwin chapter of Delta Zeta Theta," the voice said. "They call me Tank. You have to excuse my frat brother, he gets cranky in the morning."

"Fuck you, Tank," Big John grumbled as he walked away, shoving people aside as he went.

"So where did you learn to move like that?" Tank asked.

I'd been taking jiu-jitsu at the Air Force base since I was a kid, but I didn't feel like sharing my life story.

"I don't know, around," I answered vaguely.

"Around, huh?" Tank chuckled, knowing full well that I had training. "Well, my girlfriend Joanne thinks you might be a good candidate to pledge Delta."

"I don't know if I should get mixed up in all that," I said.

"We'll see," Tank countered cryptically.

Before I could respond in any way, Tank ended the conversation.

"Welcome to Baldwin High, Bobby Kovac. See you around."

Tank's second sentence was tinged with the slightest bit of threat.

"Not if he sees you first," offered Brett, desperately trying to insert himself into the conversation as Tank walked off with Joanne on his arm. The crowd dispersed.

Brett and I quickly made our way out of the Commons.

"Holy shit, Bobby!" Brett said once we were out of earshot of the general population. "That was so cool! How did you do that?"

"What the hell were you thinking, man?" I replied, deliberately evading his question. "Stepping between me and that shaved ape? You could have been killed!"

Brett actually seemed hurt by my reaction to his effort.

"But I had to," he said. "You're my friend."

And that's the kind of guy Brett was. The kind of guy that I thought I was.

* * *

After a full morning of being peppered with new kid questions, it was actually a nice break to sit with Brett and his crew at lunch. There were just so many times I could repeat the same answers to, "Are you new?" — "Where are you from?" — "Do you like it here?" Thanks to Brett's prep—"Don't ask him questions about being the new kid!"—the conversation at least wasn't about me for a while.

Brett's friends were nice enough, all physical variations of Brett, which helped take to them pretty quickly. There was a Tall Brett, a Fat Brett, and a Short Brett: Timmy, Tommy, and Ronnie respectively. They were nerds—or dorks as people called them back then—which was okay with me. As much of a jock as I was, I was still a fanboy at heart; besides comics, I loved horror movies and sci-fi, so other than my penchant for playing sports, I fit right in. And they were all funny as hell, both intentionally and unintentionally.

"Seriously, Tommy, where did you get a sandwich that big, 'Ye Olde Paul Bunyan's Sandwich Shoppe'?" Ronnie quipped, hitting the Old English silent "e's" really hard.

Fat Brett's sandwich really was huge.

"No, Ronnie, I got it from your mother's twat!" Tommy retorted, taking the lowest road possible.

"Mother's Finest Twat Sandwich Shop!" Timmy added to the exchange.

"No! Ye Olde Mother's Finest Twat Sandwich Shoppe!" Brett finished for the win.

The four of them laughed until they cried, and I was right there with them. I loved a good rank-out session.

It wasn't long before the topic of conversation turned to the morning's confrontation in the Commons. My minimally evasive actions had already taken on legendary status throughout the school. Tommy, Timmy, and Ronnie hadn't been anywhere near the occurrence, but they had misheard all about it with incredibly wrong detail.

"Did you really leap over Big John's head?!"

I tried to correct them, but you know what they say, any story worth telling is worth exaggerating. There was no bringing this one back to earth.

Now, while the rest of the world was talking about the exploits of "ol' Tricky Dick Nixon" and the suffering and atrocities of people fighting and living in Vietnam, oddly, the topic of conversation in the lunch-room was the torturous exploits of the fraternities. The actions and activities of the frat world were of disproportionate interest to Brett and his friends considering it was something they had no connection to at all besides the bullying they occasionally suffered at the hands of some of the fraternity members.

With the start of a new school year came the time for the frats to take on new pledges, and "The Bretts" informed me that there were three stages to getting into a fraternity, each more horrific than the others. To hear them tell it, most of the activities were on a level of cruelty and brutality that would make a human rights activist cringe.

First came actually being chosen to pledge a frat. I figured that would be a simple process as I had almost been asked to pledge Delta Zeta Theta that morning. But according to The Bretts, before you were actually picked you had to go through an insane, abusive interview process by the entire chapter. If you passed that and were selected to pledge the frat, the entire chapter would kick your ass and beat you with a paddle. But wait, there's more.

Next up on the hit parade of indignities came three to five weeks of what college fraternities call "hazing" but which high school frats called "dogging." So named because pledges were literally treated like dogs during this period. The dogs were expected to be at the beck and call of the entire frat, particularly each of their "pledge masters" and forced to do any sort of demeaning and humiliating thing the pledge master could think of.

During the dogging period, dogs were subjected to all types of physical and mental punishment and abuse at the hands of their future frat brothers. Besides often having to shave their heads and dress in a ridiculous, predefined manner—usually involving the fraternity colors —on any given day, a dog was expected to provide coffee and bagels to his frat members in the morning and cigarettes and gum all day long. They were also ordered to sing songs anywhere and everywhere, loudly on command, fight other fraternity pledges, eat or drink pretty much any vomit-inducing concoction presented to them, as well as endure a myriad of other sick things thought up by their miscreant prospective brothers. The local sale of pet shop goldfish would skyrocket during the dogging period, becoming a food source for would-be pledges. Any infraction or missed action done or perceived to have been done by the pledge master resulted in a demerit written into the dog's 'book' carried by the pledge at all times. These demerits were reviewed at the next frat meeting, and the offending dog would receive abuse, punches, and beatings with a paddle accordingly. Fun.

But believe it or not, that wasn't the worst of it.

If a dog didn't give up and quit along the way as a result of the intense level of abuse inflicted on him—as many did—or he wasn't blackballed by the frat for not dogging properly—which many were—he would then be treated to the grand finale, "Hell Night." And it was far worse than the name implied. To hear it told, all the horrors of being chosen to pledge the frat and the dogging period combined paled in comparison to what was in store for a dog on Hell Night. I couldn't believe that the physical abuse the pledges were subjected to was legal, let alone that anybody would allow themselves to be put through it at all, but The Bretts swore it was all true, and they weren't exaggerating. For the life of me, I couldn't figure out why anyone would voluntarily allow themselves to be treated like that.

I would soon find out.

* * *

Now, in Dayton, Ohio I had been pretty popular; and with that popularity, of course, came dating. I say, of course, because anyone who's ever gone to high school knows that it's not good looks that get dates, it's popularity. Stories are plentiful about great-looking guys or girls who couldn't get a date in school and male and female cretinous meatheads who had to fight them off with a stick. Why? More likely than not, the dateless, good-looking loser was a band or choir geek, not considered cool, one of the "smart kids" and/or had committed some social faux pas early in their life that got them the designation of having "cooties"—an incurable social disease—and they literally carried that stigma throughout their academic career. Cooties don't date. This said, all the dating I'd done, if you could call it that, would not prepare me for the moment the girl of my dreams floated past our lunch table.

"Who is that," I asked, completely mystified by her presence.

"Who are you talking about," answered Timmy, clearly not seeing what I was.

"Her," I said, now pointing to her back as she had already passed.

The guys followed the direction of my gesture.

"Angel Levitano?" Ronnie said in disbelief.

"What about her?" Brett finally chimed in.

Angel Levitano was like no girl I had ever seen before, both earthly and ethereal at the same time. While my inner self thought I was playing it cool, the slack-jawed look on my face totally betrayed me. The Bretts burst out laughing.

"And they call us dorks," Tommy laughed.

"We can't still be dorks, because ol' poker face here just lowered the bar!" Ronnie shouted, loud enough for others in the area to hear.

Now, I was fast adding the color red to my dumbfounded look just in time for Angel Levitano to turn toward the commotion. There was no way she couldn't have dealt with this kind of reaction before, but then again, these guys seemed completely unaffected by her beauty. Why was nobody else in the lunchroom seeing what I was seeing? As it turned out, Angel Levitano hadn't looked like that her entire life.

The stories are legion of Hollywood starlets and celebrities who weren't always gorgeous. Many former ugly ducklings and awkward-looking kids had blossomed into some of the most attractive women—and men—in history. This was Angel Levitano.

Born and raised in Baldwin, she entered the public school system wearing glasses, not some sleek stylish pair, but the sturdy horn rims that were the standard in the late '50s and early '60s. By the third grade, her new adult teeth that were growing in started to buck. Again, these weren't the days when parents would slap on some cute and colorful bands to space and guide the teeth in gently. This was the "you have to wait until all your adult teeth grow in and you reach puberty" days of orthodontics. That philosophy made for some long, tough years as a target of mean kids who nicknamed you things like four eyes and Bucky Beaver. And then when you finally did get braces—big, shiny, awful metal monstrosities—your new name becomes "Metal Mouth" or "Tinsel Teeth."

But then Angel's braces came off, her parents got her contact lenses, and she finally went through puberty. Unfortunately for Angel, she went through her sexual maturity late, so for a period she had to deal with having the nickname "Flatsy Patsy" added to her list. She sure wasn't anymore.

While the local boys who grew up with her since kindergarten didn't notice the incremental changes over the years, when she walked into that lunchroom past my table, I was treated to the fully-finished product. This was the only time I was glad to be the new kid. It allowed me to spot the goddess in their midst that all the other guys had been completely overlooking. Did Angel even know how beautiful she had become?

But leave it to the new kid to swallow his tongue in a goddess's presence.

There was no way Angel Levitano could have missed my love-struck condition; she smiled right at me. I knew it had nothing to do with an attraction of any kind. It was purely a pity smile for the pathetic new guy and the humiliation he was suffering through.

"Wait! Wait! Who am I?" Timmy asked, setting up his insult.

He then planted his hands on either side of his face, feigned a look of shock, and exclaimed, "A woman!!" like some Saturday morning Warner Brothers cartoon character.

Everyone howled.

"It's not the new kid is it?" Brett answered with mock innocence.

More howling from The Bretts and now a fairly-distant Angel Levitano added a giggle, a sweet, beautiful giggle.

As deep in the minus column as I knew I was, I had to meet her.

And I would.

CHAPTER FOUR

B y day two, the legend of my confrontation with Big John had reached epidemic proportions, but the truth had been twisted wildly out of control.

"I heard One Punch begged the new kid for mercy!"

As a result, the offers to pledge various fraternities started pouring in.

Tau Zeta Epsilon was the first to make their approach. They wrongly thought I was Jewish because of my last name. Kovac is an Eastern European name, but not necessarily Jewish. I wasn't interested in pledging for any frat, but not being Jewish made it a non-starter for "Red and White" anyway. I found it odd that people who had been persecuted for their religious beliefs throughout history were now rejecting me for mine. It was sort of reverse discrimination if you ask me.

In my house, any show of prejudice or bigotry was unacceptable. A half dozen kids in high school had jumped my father "because he was a Jew and caused the war"—the war being World War II. This was the same name confusion that had gotten me both invited and then uninvited to join TZE. My father "famously" had found each of his attackers and beat them up one at a time, but being on the receiving end of that kind of hatred—albeit misguided—made my father staunchly accepting of all races and creeds. That very rational philosophy was ingrained in me from the time I was a small child...and may be the reason my dad made sure I could defend myself.

So, when Beta Lambda Rho went out of their way to tell me that while they would like for me to pledge Blue and Gold, they couldn't because I was a Jew, I responded, "And proud of it!" I wasn't going to play into their overt prejudice by denying something that shouldn't have even been a consideration. This kind of open racism in high school surprised me. I knew racism existed in the military but not openly in the schools that I went to on the base at Wright-Patterson. They were fully integrated, and any kind of separation wasn't even a consideration. Long Island, on the other hand, had been a hotbed of bigotry over the past several decades. In the 1920s, the Baldwin chapter of the Ku Klux Klan would have regular cross-burnings on what used to be the golf course before Baldwin High School had been built on the poisoned land. The rotten apples clearly hadn't fallen far from the tree of the tree.

* * *

I was crossing the Commons one morning, heading to my first class, when I heard a familiar voice.

"Hey, Kovac, are you gonna pledge Delta or what?"

I turned to see Billy "Tank" Russell and a bunch of other DZO guys looking at me. This seemed a strange way for them to start their courtship.

"Didn't know I was asked."

"We've been watching you and think you are definitely Delta material."

I looked at the other Black and Green members staring at me and, with the exception of Big John who just stood there glowering, they were all nodding in agreement. I have to admit that the idea of being a part of a fraternity had a certain appeal, and the jackets were really cool. But that still wasn't enough to make me want to suffer through the dogging process.

"I appreciate being asked, Tank, but I just don't think joining a frat–"

"For a prime pledge like you, Delta is willing to sweeten the offer," Tank cut me off, ignoring anything I was saying. "Pledge DZO and we'll cut your dogging period from the usual five weeks down to two…and you won't have to shave your head like the other dogs."

Wow. Even a new kid like me realized that was an impressive offer.

"That's a hell of a deal," I said. "But I'm really not looking to join any fraternity."

"Is that right?" Tank said with a knowing grin on his face. "We'll see."

And with that, he and the other members of Delta turned and walked away, but not before Big John pointed a finger at me and shook his head; two simple gestures that spoke volumes.

By week's end, most of the other fraternities had made their approach. One by one they fell by the wayside. Besides the pledging/dogging/Hell Night horrors, being in a frat seemed to bring with it a lot of high school drama, something that had little appeal to me at that time. Not that I was too mature for those kinds of things —I wasn't—but being the new kid and just trying to make it through my last year of school felt like excitement enough at the time. Besides, their general elitist attitude that excluded anyone not in their fraternity reeked of narcissism. I liked the small group of friends I had developed, and they were the type who were definitely excluded—and sometimes persecuted—by the frats. I didn't need to be a part of that.

* * *

Back in Dayton, I had been very active in after-school sports: football every fall, hockey in the winter, and lacrosse every spring. But here I was in my senior year of high school and thanks to my father's lack of forethought, I didn't arrive in Baldwin early enough to try out for the football team. After playing football every year of my life since I started Junior Pee-Wee league when I was nine, I was suddenly teamless at a time I definitely could have used one. I may have blown football season, but I'd be damned if I would miss out on lacrosse. Long Island lacrosse was internationally known for producing some of the best teams, players, and coaches in the world.

There's a lot of speculation as to why that relatively small geographical area is such a hotbed of lacrosse talent. Some say it's because lacrosse is a Native American sport—albeit with a French name—and historically, Long Island was home to quite a number of tribes. You can't drive more than a couple of miles without hitting a town, park, building, or body of water with a native name. Massapequa town, Caumsett Park, Paumanok School, Lake Ronkonkoma; the place is lousy with them. But you'd be hard-pressed to find a single Long Island Native American if you tried. They'd all either been killed in the 1700s, forced off the island, or onto tiny reservations that most people didn't even know existed; definitely no tribal casino money there.

The more accepted reason for the glut of lacrosse stars was the large quantity of college-bound kids from this densely-populated region. Apparently, parents got hip early on to the fact that sports scholarships were a cheap way into good schools and that there was a popular—under-serviced—college sport desperate for good players. Suburban Long Island moms and dads put a lot of time, effort, and money into their children's and school's lacrosse programs, and—voila!—a college grants cash cow was born. I saw it as the single good thing about our move to Baldwin, and I wanted in on that scholarship gravy train.

Now, Brett and I had been inseparable since we met that day in early August, and we still were as we headed into the second week of school. But come Monday afternoon, I needed to stay after school and meet with the lacrosse coach, so Brett and I agreed to hang out later. We would connect again that day, but not at home as we planned.

My meeting with Coach Landers went really well. Having looked up my high school academic and sports records, he proclaimed me

"Baldwin Varsity Material" and felt confident I would make the lacrosse team in the spring. His only regret was that I had missed out on football season because "We could have used a man like you."

* * *

Ever since I was young, like a lot of suburban males, I had been a fan of cars. Particularly hot rods, muscle, and sports cars; but I was pretty well versed in anything with four wheels. Now, you can tell a lot about a person by what they drive. Back then I would kill time on long trips profiling drivers by the cars they were in. You know, the guy driving the station wagon was a family man; the guy in the flashy sports car was a ladies' man. Stereotypes for sure, but stereotypes for a reason. This said, I was not too thrilled about what my dad's silver-grey Le Sabre was saying about me.

* * *

It was a beautiful late summer day for my walk home, and I was feeling pretty good about how things had gone with the coaches and my chances of getting a coveted lacrosse scholarship. But when I turned the corner onto Brookside Avenue—the road that ran along that glorified drainage ditch I mentioned earlier—halfway up the block I saw a beater, '67 Chevy Camaro run up over the curb and sitting diagonally across the sidewalk. Primer-grey, covered in Bondo, with mismatched rims and tires; stock up front, Cragar SS rims with white lettered wide tires on the back, this car screamed trouble. And there it was, three dirtbags wearing black and white frat jackets roughing up some kid half their size. A fourth leaned against the car.

I cautiously approached, and when I got a little closer I recognized their victim. It was Brett. He was being shoved, pushed, kicked, and punched by the three lowlifes while the fourth just laughed. He was the biggest of the bunch and clearly their leader. Wearing a worn out, dirty pair of Levi's and a cut-off black and white t-shirt exposing muscular arms, for some reason he was also wearing black leather gloves. It was still summer. The assholes were harassing Brett more for

33

entertainment than anything else; less interested in actually hurting him and more in his frustration and humiliation. To Brett's credit, he was trying to fight back; but he was outmanned, outsized, and outgunned. It was a total loss situation. I continued to move toward them.

One of the reprobates gave Brett a particularly hard shove and sent him flying onto the ground, his left forearm outstretched over the curb and into the street. That's when I saw their leader's eyes light up and an evil grin spread across his pockmarked face. I knew exactly what he was going to do.

I dropped my schoolbooks and charged as the lowlife raised his tattered, blue jean-covered, Frye boot clad-leg and foot high over Brett's extended arm...and brought it down hard. First came the sickening sound of the arm snapping...then Brett's scream.

His three cronies were visibly stunned by the sudden ugly turn things had taken as Brett shrieked in pain. Fortunately, they were all so focused on my poor friend that they didn't notice me until I was right on top of them. With my arms spread wide, I quickly "clotheslined" two of them and bowled over the third with a shoulder to his chest. Then I turned on their malicious leader. He was a bruiser.

Before he had time to react, I leg-swept him, taking him to the ground, then I dropped with all my weight onto his chest and started punching him repeatedly in the face. The other dirtbags, dazed and still earthbound and seeing their biggest guy getting his ass kicked, didn't even try to get involved. When I was sure the piece of shit was incapacitated, I climbed off.

Brett was now standing and holding his broken arm across his chest, his face scrunched up from the pain.

"Let's get the fuck out of here," he said, fighting back tears.

We backed carefully away as the three other Black and White guys helped their injured brother to his feet.

"What the hell were you thinking, man?" Brett hissed under his breath as we ran. "Getting between me and those guys? You could have been killed!"

"I had to," I said with the slightest of smiles "You're my friend."

When we were a safe distance away from all involved parties, the big guy, his face a bloody mess, got brave and started shouting.

"YOU'RE A DEAD MAN, YA HEAR ME?! DEAD! NOBODY FUCKS WITH GAMMA NU!"

* * *

Delta Gamma Nu was the dirtbag frat of Baldwin's neighboring rival town, Oceanside. Formed in the '60s as an alternative fraternity for laid-back stoners, they had been persecuted mercilessly by other clubs, particularly DZO. Apparently, they weren't too happy that DGN had decided to use the same Greek letter for their frat's first name. The then president of Oceanside Delta Zeta Theta decided to make an example of this upstart fraternity and not only had all the Gamma Nu members harassed and physically abused, but he also forbade them to wear their Black and White colors publicly, even though they were legally chartered. For two long years, the stoner frat hid who they were and ran for their lives every day, until a major change occurred.

As a rule, fraternities drew their pledges from a high school pool, tenth grade and up. Delta Gamma Nu, in an effort to headhunt the best talent and protect their frat moving forward, scouted the toughest kids in junior high—seventh, eighth, and ninth-grade future badasses— offering them membership into the frat at their young age with no dogging period—only a Hell Night. With these kinds of incentives, Gamma Nu's ranks swelled, and within two years—and every year after that—Oceanside High School was inundated with the toughest tenth graders wearing Black and White frat jackets and harboring a deep-seated hatred for all fraternities... especially Delta Zeta Theta.

The miscreant who curb-stomped Brett's arm was Jimmy O'Reilly, aka Jimmy O, the president of the Oceanside chapter of Gamma Nu—the most gang-like of all the fraternities—and a legacy Black and White member. His two, scumbag older brothers were both Gamma Nu and enlisted to go to Vietnam rather than prison. Teddy O, the oldest, was killed in action in 1970 and Eddie O, ten months older than Jimmy—proverbial "Irish twins"—was still "in country" overseas. Jimmy O was following right in their Frye boot-clad footsteps to hell. A "super senior," he had been left back twice, meaning *if* he graduated this year, he would be 20 years old when it happened.

Brett's forearm was fractured in two places and put in a cast. The doctors and nurses at the hospital, suspicious of the nature of the break, grilled him about what happened, but Brett would only say that he fell while riding his bike. This was a criminal act, and Jimmy O could be brought up on charges, but Brett knew that Delta Gamma Nu would come after him if he snitched and didn't want things to get even worse for him than they already were. Besides...I would soon have my own revenge to worry about.

CHAPTER FIVE

The next day at school, I received a hero's welcome. I don't know how, but word had spread that I had beat up the toughest, nastiest member of Delta Gamma Nu and walked away without a scratch. The second Brett and I stepped onto the high school campus, people started congratulating me on my act of bravery. For the most part, my victory was just fortunate timing...but they didn't know that.

When we entered The Commons, things got even crazier. Virtually the entire area stopped, turned toward me, and cheered. Members of every fraternity and clique came over to shake my hand or slap me on the back. Jocks, freaks, geeks, smart kids, dirtbags, it seemed like everyone and anyone had, or knew someone, who had been in some way negatively affected by Jimmy O and the Gamma Nu crew. They all appreciated what I had done. Even Brett, whom everyone knew was the victim of the attack, was getting respect. Girls buzzed around him, fussing over his broken arm and cast.

"Can I sign it?" Cindy's hot Delta sorority sister Aimee asked Brett suggestively.

"Su-su-sure," he said, not exactly sure what "it" was.

With that, she took out a pink felt tip pen and wrote on his cast in flowery swirling cursive: "To Brent, Love Aimee."

"There," Aimee said, finishing dramatically with a small heart over the "i" in her name.

"My name is Brett," he said almost apologetically.

"I know," Aimee replied vacuously, then handed the pen to the next girl waiting to sign and walked off.

Brett looked at me grinning, and I shrugged. He was in heaven. I wasn't feeling too bad myself. That's when I looked over the people surrounding us and saw her. Angel Levitano was heading my way. Walking alone, she exuded a quiet confidence that most high schoolers didn't have. I pretended I hadn't spotted her and went back to talking to the kids around me, waiting for her to arrive. Finally, I would get a chance to make an impression. But it wasn't in me to play it that cool. I glanced up, expecting to see her standing there, but she wasn't. Dropping the façade, I craned my neck to look for her; she was now behind me and walking away. Throwing what was left of my poor attempt at attitude completely out the window, I ran down the hall after her.

"Hey, hi," I said when I caught up. It seemed a perfectly acceptable greeting, all things considered.

"Hey, hi," Angel replied pleasantly, confused by my approach. "Can I help you?"

She continued to walk, and I followed.

"I'm Bobby Kovac and–"

"The new kid; I know," she said.

I was still the new kid, but as least she knew I had a name.

A few members of Tau Zeta Epsilon walked by wearing their Red and White jackets.

"Hey, Kovac!" one of them shouted. "Way to go with those Gamma Nu assholes!"

I nodded, gave them a quick wave, and then continued with Angel.

"Yeah, well, I thought I'd introduce myself and—"

"What was that about," she asked.

Finally, I had an opening with this amazing girl.

"I beat up these four guys in Black and White pretty good yesterday," I bragged, out to impress.

"So you're one of those frat guys?" Angel asked, but she said the words "frat guys" like she had tasted something disgusting.

Clearly, my heroics weren't going to get me anywhere with this girl, so I immediately started to backpedal.

"Who me? No, I ju—"

Two dirtbag guys from Black and Blue came up behind me and slapped me hard on the back.

"Nice going, new kid," one of them said without an ounce of enthusiasm.

"Beta Kappa Phi's got your back," said the other, banging a new soft pack of Camel non-filters on the palm of his hand.

Why they did that when they walked down the halls in school I still don't know; probably because that's what bad kids do: pull out their cigarette packs and wave them around to show off. Back then, smoking was still considered cool. I didn't bother to respond to the "pack banger" and continued my struggling conversation with Angel.

"No, no," I said, too defensively. "I'm not in a fraternity. Some guys were beating up my friend—they broke his arm—so I had to step in and help him."

"You're a good friend," she conceded.

"Nice work, Kovac!" someone yelled; this time it was a member of Beta Lambda Rho.

I was running 50/50 on being called new kid or by my name.

"Thanks," I shouted back hurriedly.

I needed to get past this bump in the road with Angel, and for some reason, all of these platitudes weren't helping.

"I can see you've got fans to attend to; I've got to get to class," Angel said matter-of-factly.

And with that, she turned and walked away.

"See you around sometime...?" I said trying to be casual, but it was a bit too loud; and by the end of the sentence, I had drifted off, and it had turned into a needy question.

"Are you sure?" Angel said with a smile as she continued walking.

I couldn't figure out what had just happened. Everyone else was so impressed.

"Hey, Bobby!" I heard Brett shout from down the hall.

I turned to see him still in all his glory, having his cast signed by more girls.

"Are you comin' or what?!"

"I'm coming, I'm coming," I said as I jogged back down the hall to join him.

"How did it go?" Brett asked.

His new cast was covered with girls' signatures, mostly signed to "Brent."

"Not great, Brent," I said. "I went over to her a zero, and now I may be less than zero."

"So there was some movement?" Brett said with a smirk.

We both laughed.

* * *

By lunchtime, my exploits with Gamma Nu had even raised the cred
of the other Bretts. Tommy, Timmy, and Ronnie had gone from being
completely invisible to "those guys who sit with the new kid." Sure, it
was only a slight upgrade, but they seemed pretty pleased by it.

We were clowning around, eating our lunch, and coming up with
non-sequiturs…

"Which is longer, California or by train?" I offered. An oldie but a
goodie.

"What's the difference between a duck?" Timmy added.

"Do you walk to school or take your lunch?" Ronnie shot back.

"I asked one of the Theta girls that question," Tommy said. "I figured
it would be a funny icebreaker."

"So what happened?" Brett asked.

"She looked at me dead serious and said, 'No, I live across the street,'
then walked away," Tommy answered.

We all broke up laughing.

"That's the only possible answer!" Brett concluded.

"Great pickup line, by the way," I said, and the laughter continued.

Suddenly, The Bretts' laughter stopped, and their collective eyes went
wide.

"Uh-oh," Tommy said.

"What?" I asked, reacting to Fat Brett's tone.

Brett's and my backs were to the room; Tommy, Timmy, and Ronnie
were sitting across from us.

"Behind you," Ronnie said with concern, looking past me.

"Shit," Timmy added.

41

I spun around to see Tank and the largest gathering of DZO members I'd seen so far—almost two-dozen guys—heading toward our table. Seeing an approaching army—their intent unclear—all of the nearby lunch tables scattered, as did Tommy, Timmy, and Ronnie. Once again, Brett stood by my side. With his broken arm, he was now more of a liability than ever, but still…

"That's a lot of Black and Green," he whispered to me nervously.

"I'll handle Tank, you take care of the rest," I said with a wink. I wasn't really that concerned. Besides passing on their offer to pledge, I hadn't done anything to rub them the wrong way…except to Big John.

"You are one crazy fucker, Kovac," Tank shouted from halfway across the lunchroom.

Back then, guys referred to each other more often than not by their last names. I don't know why, but it definitely felt more masculine to talk to each other that way.

"Why's that?" I shouted back, pretty sure I knew exactly what he was talking about.

"Taking on four Gamma Nu guys on your own?" Tank said.

He and the rest of Delta now had Brett and me surrounded.

"Had to be done," I said. "My friend needed me."

Brett smiled.

"You took out Jimmy O," Tank said, "Nice."

The other DZO members nodded their approval and smiled along with him. Except for One Punch, of course.

It turned out that Jimmy O and Gamma Nu had been a major thorn in the side of not only Oceanside Delta but the Baldwin chapter, as well.

"Are you sure you don't want to pledge Delta?" Tank continued. "Doing what you did to Jimmy O doesn't just give you an enemy, it gives you 45 enemies. All Black and White are gunning for you now."

"You're gonna need some brothers," Big John added begrudgingly.

I still wasn't getting it.

"I appreciate what you're offering, but I got things under control."

"Sure," Tank said with a wry smile. "You let me know when you change your mind."

I was starting to get the feeling that he didn't really care what I had to say about anything.

With that, Tank, Big John, and the Black and Green pack turned as one and headed back out of the lunchroom.

"Wow," Brett said.

"Yeah, wow," I said absentmindedly. The true weight of everything happening was beginning to sink in.

CHAPTER SIX

I t's funny how at traumatic moments in your life you remember everything leading up to it so vividly. The sounds, the colors, the conversation, the smell of the air, everything around you, it all gets seared into your memory. Like it's your mind's way of saying, "Don't you ever forget."

After school, Brett and I met up to walk home as usual. It was one of those late summer days that lets you know fall is at the doorstep: crisp, clear, blue skies, high clouds, still warm, but just a hint of sweet coolness in the air. Perfect.

I clearly remember our discussion that day. We were talking about how the glitter rock movement of the time with Alice Cooper, David Bowie, T. Rex, and others was starting to dominate the hard rock scene. There were even rumors of a band out of the city called the New York Dolls who, literally dressing and looking like women, were really pushing the boundaries of sexuality and what my immature mind was capable of dealing with. While Brett loved the excitement and provocation of the look and sound, as a pretty homophobic jock, I definitely felt threatened by "men that looked like women." Longer hair had been accepted by the masses by that time—even normal kids had hair past their ears—but these bands were pushing the boundaries of male femininity with their makeup, outrageous clothing, and insanely long hair. For an Air Force brat like myself, this was just too hard a pill to swallow. There was one glitter band called Mott the Hoople that had just released a single called "All the Young Dudes" that both Brett and I agreed was really cool. To my younger homophobic self, at least their lead singer Ian Hunter didn't look like he was gay.

Brett and I had a pretty regular route we took home from school each day. Through the field by the tennis courts, across The Brook, through the parking lot behind the synagogue where we'd occasionally see members of Tau Zeta Epsilon dressed up in suits and ties attending services, then out onto Brookside Avenue. We'd follow Brookside pretty much all the way to where we lived, but that day was so nice and the conversation so passionate, we took a slightly longer route and veered a bit west onto Forest Avenue. That road would take us to the far end of Ardmore road, a couple of blocks farther from our houses, but it had a lot less traffic than Brookside.

"Just because those guys wear makeup doesn't mean they're fags," Brett said.

"Well, it doesn't mean they're macho," I responded. "I saw a picture of that David Bowie in *Creem* magazine on his knees in front of his guitar player pretending to blow him!"

I figured I had Brett there.

"Pretending. He's just fucking with your head, man," Brett said. "Have you seen pictures of Bowie's wife, Angie? She's hot...and they have a baby boy named Zowie!"

"Zowie Bowie?" I said, really confused. "What kind of a stupid na–"

We suddenly became aware of the roar of an un-muffled car engine behind us. Jimmy O's beater Camaro violently jumped the curb onto the sidewalk blocking our way. The car doors opened and Jimmy and the three other Gamma Nu dirtbags we had the altercation with the day before climbed out.

"Now you're fucked," Jimmy O said, waving a bat in one of his black leather-gloved hands.

Sure, I had beaten those four assholes before, but then I had the element of surprise. I wasn't feeling as confident about my chance of a repeat with them not only ready for me but armed.

"Let's go!" I said to Brett, and we turned and ran in opposite directions.

Just then two more cars roared up, one driving over the sidewalk blocking each of our exits and the other pulling alongside of us on the street, boxing us in. At least ten more members of Black and White, carrying pipes, bats, chains, and knives piled out. We really were fucked.

"Follow me!" Brett yelled and, using his good arm, pulled me toward the house we were in front of.

With the pack of Black and White members close behind, we ran into the backyard and kept running.

As it turned out, being chased by bullies was something Brett had way too much experience with. Not necessarily this quantity of bullies, but bullies just the same. Bored asshole troublemakers with no one specific to harass, practice their shitty craft by hassling random wimpy kids. From time to time, their target was Brett.

So regular were these fucked up occurrences that Brett and his friends actually did practice runs, cutting through the backyards of houses. On any given night—weather permitting—The Bretts would dodge, jump, duck, and dive, over through, and under various neighborhood fences, dogs, and lawn furniture as fast as they could, all the while imagining they were being chased by some predator. Not only did they get exceptionally good at doing this, but they also came to really know their way through most of the backyards in the surrounding neighborhoods. Even with his one arm in a cast Brett still had us flying through the properties. In other words, we had the home-field advantage.

We exited the last yard with a big lead. After a series of evasive moves, we finally tucked ourselves under the Centennial Avenue overpass, crouching in the dry stream-bed of Brookside Avenue. Brett and I waited, breathing heavily, not saying a word, listening for any sign of Gamma Nu.

Finally, in the distance, we heard the approaching rumble of the beater Camaro, its Cherry Bomb glass-pack mufflers doing their job, distorting the sound of the "mom and pop" Chevy small block into approaching thunder. And then a voice shouting over the rumble joined the fray. It was Jimmy O's.

"I'M GONNA FIND YOU, CUNT-VACS!"

The car and the rumble slowly got closer, and Jimmy continued to yell.

"I'M GONNA FIND YOU!"

Closer.

"I'M GONNA FIND YOU, CUNT-VACS…"

Then it was right on top of us. The echo under the overpass amplified the rumble of the Camaro to a roar.

"…AND WHEN I DO, I'M GONNA SPLIT YOUR HEAD OPEN LIKE A MELON!"

Jimmy O had no idea we were literally right underneath him. His car crossed over our heads and continued to drive on.

"YOU HEAR ME? I'M GONNA FIND YOU!"

The sound of the car and Jimmy O's voice trailed off in the distance.

"YOU'RE A DEAD MAN, CUNT-VACS!"

When the sounds of the Camaro and Jimmy O's voice had trailed off completely…and as "YOU'RE DEAD!" echoed ominously within the relative safety of our secluded hideout…Brett and I finally felt it was safe to talk.

"Damn, Bobby, that was close," Brett half-whispered, still playing it cautious.

"You saved my ass, man," I said.

"Consider us even," Brett said with a sigh of relief.

Just in case Gamma Nu was still cruising the area, we decided to follow the dry stream-bed behind the houses all the way to Suicide Hill, not for fun, but for survival. Not saying a word the entire way—I think we were both processing the whole insane experience—we then cut through The Woods, across Clyde Field, and through the yards of the houses near our homes. It would be the last time we did that together. When we finally got to Brett's house, we broke our silence.

"I'm definitely going to need some fraternity brothers," I said.

"Ya think?" Brett said in a perfect deadpan.

And we laughed, neither of us truly realizing that our troubles with Delta Gamma Nu had only just begun.

CHAPTER SEVEN

As promised, Delta Zeta Theta—my fraternity of choice for obvious reasons—stuck to their offer of a shortened dogging period and no mandatory head shaving, but there was still the required interview. The Bretts warned me that things could get rough and that there would be some paddling, but I didn't think for a minute it was something I couldn't handle. They had asked me to pledge Delta; it shouldn't be more than a formality.

The interviews were held at the monthly DZO meeting in the basement of Big John's parents' house. They wouldn't be home, so some drinking and smoking was a guarantee. I was never much of a partier, but I was looking forward to what I thought would be my first frat party when my dad dropped me off.

"Don't do anything that I wouldn't do," he said with a broad knowing chuckle and a wink. It was his standard send-off anytime he brought me anywhere, and he sometimes said it in front of my friends, which just added to the "dadness" of the drop-off. I couldn't wait to get my driver's license.

Big John's house was in an older part of town. It sat in a row of narrow two-story classic 1940s-era homes, each with a small porch in the front and a detached garage in the back. The driveways ran along the right side of the house with the left side of each neighbor's home pretty much right on top of it. This was the way the entire neighborhood was built, each with just a small, fenced yard in the back and no front lawn to speak of. It was pretty claustrophobic.

Wearing the required potential pledge interview attire—dress slacks, shoes, and a button-down collared shirt with a tie—I headed down the driveway. I was told to use the back door, but I stopped short when I ran into five other guys from school standing in a line along the side of the house in the dark. Each was dressed to impress, and all looked extremely nervous. I was older than the others by a couple of years, the typical pledge being inducted in his sophomore year of high school.

"What's going on?" I asked, wondering why the hell they would be standing outside. It was early fall and already getting a bit chilly at night.

"Listen," someone said with more than a little foreboding.

I tuned into what I should have already been hearing; it sounded like there was a riot going on in the basement.

"What the hell is that?" I asked, confused by the muffled combination of yelling, laughing, and screaming coming from below.

"Johnny Walsh," responded Joey "Crack" Wolensky. "They're taking us in one at a time, and he was the first to go down."

Joey Crack was so nicknamed not because he did crack—that stuff didn't even exist until the early '80s—but because one day he bent over to pick something up in class, and being a pretty big guy, his shirt pulled out of the back of his fashionable, low-cut jeans. The crack of his ass rose out of his waistband like a giant hairy millipede. I'm told it was terrifying. As I said, nicknames are rarely flattering.

Whatever it was they were doing to Johnny, I was sure it had nothing to do with me. I was the guy every frat wanted; that typical hazing bullshit was for other pledges, not me.

When the insanity coming from the basement finally stopped, there was a long, uncomfortable silence, then the sound of the backdoor to the house opening. It needed to be oiled.

Big John Russo stepped out into the driveway. There was no sign of Johnny Walsh.

"Next victim," he said without the slightest bit of humor. Nobody ever accused Big John of being whimsical.

The others hesitated, but I stepped boldly forward.

"Let's get this over with," I said, knowing I was a made man.

"Oh, no," Big John said with a shark-like grin, "I'm saving you for last."

I was still so cocksure of my strong position with DZO that I didn't read anything into that grin. I should have.

One by one, each of the interviewees was taken down to the basement, and the madness from below would float up and outside. After a time it would end, and there would be a short but ominous silence. Then the back door would creak open again, Big John would step out, and another victim would be brought in. By the time they finally got to me, I was chilled to the bone from the night air and anxious to get inside.

"Time's up, Cunt-vacs," Big John said, again with the shark teeth. "You get special treatment."

"It's about time," I said. "I'm freezing out here."

"Oh, it's plenty warm downstairs," Big John said reassuringly. "Come on in."

That was the moment I knew something wasn't right. Big John Russo was incapable of human kindness.

As I descended the wooden steps into the dark, unfinished basement with One Punch behind me, the first thing that struck me was the smell of beer, smoke, and sweaty bodies carried up on a moist wave of heat. Not the kind of heat you get from a radiator but from too many people being too active in too small a space for too long. It was suffocating.

There were DZO members packed right to the bottom of the staircase; every Baldwin chapter member was there. They parted to let me pass when I reached the bottom step. Without warning, Big John shoved me violently into the center of the circle of Black and Green only dimly lit by candlelight.

"ON YOUR KNEES, PROSPECT!" Big John boomed.

Was he kidding? I wasn't getting on my knees for anybody. Then something struck me hard across the back of my legs, taking them out from under me and bringing me to the place I had just told myself that I wouldn't go.

Then it began.

The DZO members closed in around me, and Tank Russell stepped forward and took control of the interview.

"DELTA ZETA THETA, THIS IS BOBBY KOVAC!" Tank shouted like a marine drill sergeant. "POTENTIAL PLEDGE KOVAC, MEET…"

And with that, at a way too rapid pace, he barked out all of the frat members' names one after the other. There had to be 30 of them. When he got to the last one…

"NOW REPEAT THEIR NAMES BACK TO ME!" Tank bellowed.

Besides Tank and Big John, I knew virtually none of the other members; and at the speed Tank had recited them, I barely managed to get out three or four. The second I missed the first one, the entire fraternity erupted.

"WRONG!" they said in unison and rained down a hail of punches and kicks upon me. Not the kind that did any real damage but hurt.

"AGAIN!" Tank yelled. "DO IT AGAIN!"

So, I tried but didn't get much further than before...

"WRONG!" they all screamed again, kicking and punching me with abandon.

"DO IT AGAIN!"

"But I can't remember their names!" I said, stupidly trying to interject logic into an insanely illogical ritual.

"AGAIN!" Tank roared.

So I began...

"Tank, Big John, Frankie the Mouth, Jerry...Stones?"

"WRONG!"

More punches and kicks.

"DO IT AGAIN!"

This went on for at least ten minutes until Tank suddenly shifted gears and everyone in the room began shouting insane rapid-fire questions at me.

"ARE YOU WILLING TO DEFEND THE DELTA COLORS TO THE DEATH IF YOU MUST!?"

"To the death?" I answered stupidly.

"WRONG ANSWER!"

Punches and kicks.

"CAN WE HAVE KEG PARTIES AT YOUR HOUSE!?"

"I'd have to ask my par–"

"WRONG ANSWER!"

Punches and kicks.

"IF YOU WERE NAKED IN A DESERT WITH ONLY YOUR DELTA COLORS AND YOU HAD TO TAKE A SHIT, WHAT WOULD YOU USE TO WIPE YOUR ASS!?"

"My hand?" I quickly said, thinking that I was finally catching on.

"WHAT KIND OF DISGUSTING ANIMAL WIPES HIS ASS WITH HIS HAND!?"

Punches and kicks.

"DO YOU WALK TO SCHOOL OR TAKE YOUR LUNCH?!"

"I live across the street?" I said in desperation.

There was a slight, confused pause.

"But you don't live across the str–," Tank started to say but then re-grouped. "WRONG ANSWER!"

Punches and kicks.

This went on for another ten minutes or so but felt like forever until I was suddenly and violently yanked to my feet and shoved through the pack back toward the stairs.

"Wait up in the kitchen with the others," Tank said. "We'll make our decision."

"And don't fucking touch my parents' food," Big John added.

He was such a dutiful son.

Dazed, confused, and beaten up, I walked into the kitchen and found the others each in a similar state, standing and sitting around.

"What the fuck was that about?" I asked the room.

"That was the interview," Joey Crack said. "Now they vote on who gets to pledge Delta."

"Well, I guess that wasn't too bad," I said. "Insane, but not too bad."

"Sure, but that's before you get picked," said one of the other prospects that I didn't yet know.

"It's when you're accepted as a pledge that shit gets really dark," Crack added.

"What do you mean by dark?" I asked.

Before anybody could answer me....

"WOLENSKY, CREEDER, STEFKO...KOVAC, YOU MADE THE CUT!" Big John's voice filled the room. "YOU OTHER TWO LOSERS GET THE FUCK OUT OF MY HOUSE!"

Me, Crack, Joey "Drummer Boy" Stefko, and Marky "Mofo" Creeder looked at one another not sure what was going to happen next. The other two guys—Johnny Walsh and some other guy whose name I never did learn—seemed almost relieved to not have their names called. As bad as they had wanted to join DZO, the implied threat of membership had completely wiped away all desire.

"DELTA DOGS, GET YOUR ASSES DOWNSTAIRS. NOW!"

The four of us descended the basement staircase, reentered the angry circle, and once again were forced to our knees. This time I really took in my surroundings. There were empty beer cans and cigarette butts everywhere, and the smell of ragweed marijuana mixed with the stench of sweat, beer, farts, and B.O. saturated the room. Those guys were wasted. This time Tank calmly—and slowly—introduced the various frat officers; we weren't asked to repeat their names.

"And now each of you will be assigned a pledge master for the duration of your dogging period," Tank continued. "While you must answer to every member of DZO during this time, your pledge master will be in charge of overseeing your hazing. He will issue demerits as needed and serve up the appropriate punishment when necessary. And when I say 'appropriate' I mean...anything fucking goes!"

This last statement made the room roar with laughter.

Still kneeling, one by one each of us was introduced to our personal pledge master. When it was my turn...

"Kovac," Tank said, "as you have a reduced dogging period that won't start for a few weeks and are considered a prime pledge, I wanted to be sure to assign the perfect pledge master for the short time you will be a dog: the Baldwin chapter of DZO's sergeant-at-arms, Big John Russo."

As the room cheered, Big John Russo and his shark grin stepped up in front of me. He definitely had an unnatural amount of teeth.

"Hello, *dog*," Big John said ominously. Then he rocked me with an open hand slap across my face so hard it spun my head and made blood spurt from my nose. There was nothing playful about it.

Reeling, I tried to get to my feet to retaliate, but I was quickly surrounded by Delta members and forced back to my knees.

"I said anything goes," Tank whispered into my ear ominously, then, "SHAVE 'EM!"

Each of the pledge masters, now brandishing a hair buzzer, switched them on and prepared to shave their dog's head bald. The buzzing sound filled the room like a swarm of bees.

When Big John grabbed my head, I yelled, "You said no head shaving!"

"Let him go," Tank said.

Big John held my head tightly by my hair and brought the buzzer closer to my scalp.

"BIG JOHN!" Tank barked.

"This is the last special treatment you get, Cunt-vacs," Big John breathed angrily in my ear. "You're mine."

Then he roughly shoved my head away and turned off his buzzer.

The other three pledge masters laid into their dog's heads, shaving them down to the skull, none too gently or neatly either. Some of their heads were bleeding from the rough treatment.

When they were finished and the DZO congregation was done cheering and laughing at the pledges' humiliation, Tank continued with the ceremony.

"James Wolensky…Joseph Stefko…Mark Creeder…and Robert Kovac," Tank said solemnly, "you have each been accepted to pledge Delta Zeta Theta."

As he said each dog's name, he fastened a DZO "pledge pin" to their shirt.

"Wolensky, Stefko, and Creeder, your dogging period officially starts tomorrow; Kovac, hell awaits you in three weeks. Good luck," Tank added.

I wasn't sure how I felt about what had just gone on. The ridicule, Big John hitting me in the face, and the threats were way more than I expected; I was close to blowing the entire thing off. I got up and started to leave when I heard from behind me...

"Where do you think you're going, dog?"

It was Big John. Several members of the frat grabbed me, pulled me back to the center of the room, and forcibly bent me over. I could see that the other three pledges were already being held in this vulnerable position.

"PLEDGE MASTERS!" Tank shouted, "YOU GET FIVE SHOTS EACH!"

And with that, Big John and the three other DZO pledge masters, brandishing paddles, administered their dog his "shots." This was far more brutal than you can imagine.

First of all, the word paddle is way too innocent a word to describe these weapons of torment used by fraternities on their pledges for initiation. It conjures up images of ping-pong and rowboats, which is probably where they originated. Over the years, the fraternity paddle had mutated into something more in line with a cricket bat, which I'm sure would have been used if they knew the sport existed. The paddles were made from scratch with the sole purpose of inflicting maximum pain.

Inspired by the punishment exacted upon them during their initiations, fraternity members spent an inordinate amount of time and effort creating the most devastating paddle to use on future pledges. And I use the word "paddle" loosely.

Starting with the hardest of woods—mahogany, oak, cherry, or the like were the trees of choice—frat members would cut a wide thick piece using their father's tools. Some would even bring their "project" into the wood shop at school. Then they would sand and shape their "board of education" into an elongated paddle-like shape, creating the perfect weapon of torment.

Many tricks and a lot of thought went into increasing the paddle's destructive abilities. The only rule was that it couldn't be made out of anything but wood, though some did experiment with adding weights and nail heads. If only they had put as much effort into their schoolwork.

Some believed the paddle needed to be highly polished so it could more efficiently slice through the air. Others swore it had to be rough sanded for more holding power on impact. Still others would drill a series of holes for better airflow and less air resistance, though the number of holes and best pattern were hotly debated. Aerodynamics was the one science class that had fraternity members riveted. One thing was always certain: getting paddled hurt like hell.

While the other three pledge masters swung their paddles at their dog's vulnerable buttocks using a traditional baseball style swing—"He's going for the fence!"—Big John Russo was out to exact his revenge for the humiliation he suffered at my hands that first day of school. As the other DZO members held me firmly in place, Big John took a running start from across the room, giving additional velocity to each of the five shots. The pain was blinding.

When they were finished, leaving each of us curled up on the floor in pain, Tank made his final pronouncement:

"All right, dogs, you are now official Delta Zeta Theta pledges. But this is only the beginning. Your dogging period will be brutal, and there will be plenty more paddling and beatings to come. If you can't take it…then I guess you're just not DZO material."

Again, the room roared with laughter. I would find out why.

"Now run home," Tank continued. "And by run, I mean literally run. We will be driving around looking for each one of you; if we find you, we're going to beat your ass and dog you the rest of the way to your house! NOW GO!"

I couldn't believe what I was hearing.

Accompanied by a chant of "GO, DOGS, GO!" from the entire frat membership, the four of us limped up the stairs and out onto the street. I was pissed.

"Holy fuck, that hurt!" Creeder said.

"And it's only gonna get worse," Stefko added.

"It's gonna get even fucking worse right now if we don't haul ass the hell out of here," Crack said.

"Fuck that," I said. "I'm not running from my own damn frat."

I finished my proclamation to no one, as the other three had already taken off.

There was no way I was going to run home. I was joining Delta for protection, not to get my ass kicked. With brothers like that, who needed enemies? I made up my mind right then and there, I would not be dogging for Delta Zeta Theta. So I started "walking."

Limping down the road, still feeling the pain from Big John's paddling —and knowing it was going to feel a hell of a lot worse tomorrow—I was lost in confusing thoughts about how strange this new town was. I was raised on a military base, yet this place was far more war-like and violent than anything I had ever known. What was wrong with these people?

I couldn't have gotten more than a few blocks away when a station wagon filled with dark bodies screeched to a halt in the street right in front of me. I guessed Tank and Big John weren't making idle threats about beating up their own pledges. I readied myself for the attack, but when the car doors opened, out poured a squad of Delta Gamma Nu members decked out in black and white. Jimmy O was the last to

61

slowly get out of the car, taking a long, deep drag on a more than half-smoked cigarette he held in the fingers of his black leather glove.

"I guess all those years of being an altar boy paid off, even if I did have to put up with the occasional Father Francis ass grab," he said, timing the words perfectly with his exhale. "God has answered my prayers… and now you're gonna get to meet him."

I was completely out of options.

Just as suddenly as Jimmy O and company had arrived, two carloads filled with Delta members screeched up and piled out behind me, outnumbering Gamma Nu two to one. *This was the brotherhood.*

"You lost, O'Reilly?" Tank asked.

"Not at all, Russell," Jimmy O replied. "I found what I'm looking for."

"Well, maybe you better look again," Tank said, pointing to the Delta pledge pin on my shirt. "This is Bobby Kovac; he's dogging DZO, and he's protected. Any of you Gamma Nu pieces of shit lay a hand on him, every chapter of Delta will come down on your frat hard."

Apparently, there was an unwritten law among the fraternities about targeting dogs during their hazing period.

"So, let me do the simple math for you dumb fucks," Tank continued. "You've got what, a total of 75 current members of Gamma Nu at your disposal? Well, there are more than 300 active members of Delta Zeta Theta ready to go. That's four of us to each one of you dirtbag assholes…and we got you two-to-one on our turf right now."

Tank paused for dramatic effect and let the numbers sink in. Jimmy O seemed to be considering the odds.

"Complex math," Jimmy O finally said. "Very impressive."

Jimmy O took another long drag from his non-filtered cigarette, burning it to the nub. He then slowly exhaled as he flicked the cigarette butt in my direction, deftly giving me the middle finger on his gloved hand at the same time.

"There's plenty of time," he said as he got back into the car. "I'll be seeing you around...Cunt-vacs."

"That's right, asshole. Get back in your mommy's car and drive the fuck out of here before they have to carry you out," Tank said, getting in the final word.

Jimmy O's toadies followed, then they slowly drove off.

I couldn't believe I had been saved. My relief was tangible.

"Thank you guys so much," I gushed. "I thought I was dead."

"I told you that you were gonna need some brothers," Big John said.

"Get in the car, Bobby," Tank said somberly. "We're driving you home."

As I drove through town in a car filled with my future DZO brothers, and another car following close behind to make sure I was safe, at that moment I knew I wasn't going anywhere. They could dog me as long and hard as they wanted; I was joining Delta Zeta Theta.

CHAPTER EIGHT

When it finally started, dogging wasn't as bad as they said it would be…it was so much worse. I had been watching what the other pledges were suffering through for a few weeks and dreading what would happen when Big John finally got his hands on me…and with good reason.

That first day of my hazing, I arrived extra early, ready for anything. I knew the 4-1-1 on what was expected of a Delta pledge, and I had everything in order. Wearing a white shirt, black pants, highly-polished black shoes, green suspenders, and a green bow tie—the DZO colors—I had on an empty backpack and my "dogging kit"—a metal lunch box—well-stocked. It was filled with the required supplies. If any member of the frat asked for a piece of gum, a cigarette, or wanted their shoes shined and a dog wasn't ready to oblige, it meant a demerit put in their "dogging book"—also carried in the kit. Each demerit equaled a shot from your pledge master at the next meeting and an actual brick put in your backpack to lug around for the rest of the day. If you got too many demerits, you could be lugging around a backpack full of bricks; even worse, you might be blackballed from the frat. Once a dog was blackballed, no other fraternity would even consider pledging him.

Besides the obligatory daily uniform and supplies, I also had to have coffee and buttered rolls—a high school favorite—ready for all the DZO officers upon their arrival at school. No dog was allowed to make eye contact with any frat member unless spoken to, and I had to recite a very specific greeting when approached:

> Greetings Mr. (DZO brother's name here), most excelled brother of Delta Zeta Theta Fraternity. I am but a humble dog who most joyfully awaits your every command, sir.

I still remember it all these years later. I said it enough times during my two-week dogging period; and if I forgot to say it or said it wrong, I got hard smacked in the face, a demerit in my dogging book, and a brick in my backpack. So yeah...I still remember it.

Yet, all these things—the clothes, the food, the greeting, the shoeshines—were the least humiliating of the stupidity they put us dogs through. At any moment—and I mean any—if a frat brother yelled, "Air raid drill!" every pledge within earshot had to drop to the ground and ball up with our hands covering our heads. If any member of DZO yelled, "Fleas!" we had to roll around and scratch like a dog. Not like a pledge dog...like a literal dog. And then there was the public singing. Anytime, anywhere—even in the middle of a class—on command, a dog had to break into a song (of their frat brother's choosing) at the top of his lungs until told he could stop. It was embarrassing. But it wasn't worse than the physical abuse.

One day Drummer Boy walked into school with the skin from the tip to the bridge of his nose scraped raw.

"What the hell happened, Joey?" I asked.

"The Mouth made me push a cigarette down the length of the shopping center with my nose," he answered.

Frankie the Mouth was Stefko's pledge master.

"That's like two blocks!" I said in sheer disbelief.

"More like three," Joey said, blood dripping from the end of his nose. "I gotta go to the nurse."

Physical abuse.

* * *

Besides earned paddles and smacks, there were spontaneous beatings administered, especially at fraternity meetings. At any time—for no reason at all—a dog could be punched, kicked, slapped, and more, and we just had to stand there and take it. Sometimes we would be ordered to wrestle or fight another pledge.

Now some of the fraternity brothers went easy on us with this stuff. They remembered what it was like when they were dogged and didn't want to inflict that kind of pain and humiliation on anybody else. But for every one of those, there were two Big Johns ready to make up for the others' kindness in spades, which brings me to the eating and drinking challenges...

Dogs were attached to their pledge masters from morning until night —unless dismissed earlier—and often required to hang out after school for extra dogging time. Now pledges were expected to ingest whatever their pledge master commanded. This could include anything from massive amounts of alcohol to some sickening concoction they whipped up. Usually produced in the kitchen of their home, they would mix together anything "edible" they could find—ketchup, mustard, hot sauce, cooking oil, soy sauce, and more—and force the dog to down every last drop with the sole intention of making him sick and/or vomit. It was beyond awful.

As terrible as all this was and as hard as Big John rode me—and he did make my dogging life miserable—I suffered through every indignity Delta put upon me, rarely getting a demerit. I didn't want to give DZO any reason to blackball me. That would mean I'd be left to protect myself against the vengeful Jimmy O and Delta Gamma Nu, who were just waiting for me to fail.

* * *

Leaving for school early every morning and coming home after dark—often beaten up, sick to my stomach, and/or drunk—my mom became very concerned for my wellbeing...as she should have. I hid things as best I could from my parents, but moms have this other sense. One day when I walked in particularly late, looking exceptionally trashed, she confronted me.

"Robert Henry Kovac, what in the H-E-double hockey sticks is going on?" she demanded.

My mom never cursed. Using my middle name and brushing dangerously close to profanity meant she was really upset.

Dancing around the truth, I tried to explain the unexplainable to her without actually telling her anything. Fortunately, my dad stepped in to defend me. He had been in a college fraternity and thought he understood the hazing thing. He had told me tales of what his college fraternity had done to him. What he dealt with at his university bore only the slightest resemblance to what those high school frat miscreants were putting me through.

"Oh, let him be, Judy," he said. "Hazing builds character."

The verb I would have used was "destroys," but I kept silent.

"Besides," my father continued, "fraternities do a lot of good for their communities."

Really? Not any of those high school hoodlums. But such was the perception of the high school fraternities. Since college frats did community work, so must the high school ones. Wrong.

But my mom wasn't giving up that easily. Being a housewife—few women weren't in the early '70s—while my father spent his days at the Grumman plant, she interacted with the other neighbors and her new friends.

"Some of the girls are telling me that this dogging thing can get out of control," my mom pushed back.

So I did what I would do for weeks and months to come…I lied through my teeth.

"Stop being such a worrywart, Mom," I said. "It's nothing; I'm fine."

"You see, Judy," my dad interjected, "it's just high school hijinks."

"I don't know…," my mom said, caving reluctantly.

This was only the first of many lies I would tell my parents to hide the bruises, illnesses, inebriation, and a myriad of other maladies my being involved with DZO would bring. And the worst was yet to come.

CHAPTER NINE

During my two-week dogging period, I really didn't get to see much of Brett. I had to be up extra early every morning to load my dogging kit with essentials and pick up coffee and buttered rolls at the local deli for my fraternity leaders. Not being ready and waiting at school with any of these things when they arrived was an instant demerit, so I was out each day before dawn. Brett liked me a lot but not enough to suffer through that with me, which I completely understood. I wouldn't have done it for him either.

At lunch, I was expected to sit with and be abused by my DZO brothers—so that killed any hang time with The Bretts, as well. And every day after school—sometimes until night—I was expected to be Big John's lackey to torment until he got tired…which he rarely did. So, it was only on the rarest of occasions that Brett and I got to hang out. But he was totally cool about it. We both knew it would soon be over, then his best friend would officially be a member of Delta Zeta Theta. Brett could already see his star rising just by association. Dreams of sorority girls and cheerleaders calling him by his correct name filled his head.

* * *

Toward the end of my dogging period, I was really put to the test. I had suffered through and survived every bit of abuse and stupidity that Big John and my future DZO brothers had thrown at me without getting more than a few demerits in my book…until one life-changing morning in the high school Commons. The usual insanity was ensuing with the various frats barking out orders to their pledges and putting them through the paces of dogging life. It's amazing that the school authorities allowed it to go on.

"Where's my coffee?!"

"Shine my shoes!"

"AIR RAID!"

"Grab her tits!"

Yeah…that was a thing.

A pledge master could order his dog to grab some unsuspecting girl's breasts. It wasn't considered sexual assault back then like it should have been; it was *hijinks*. Usually, the victim was a member of the frat's sister sorority who, while upset, knew the deal and would do no more than scream and slap the offending pledge, much to the amusement of the other fraternity and sorority members. The sororities were in the midst of their version of dogging their own pledges as well, so the whole thing had a certain give and take to it.

While my fellow pledges and I were being put through our daily humiliations, Angel Levitano happened to walk by. This was the first time I'd run into her since I started dogging; looking and acting this way was not how I wanted her to see me. Angel spotted me and smiled; I'm sure more for my appearance and behavior than anything else. I was so embarrassed I couldn't control my reaction: I blushed… and Big John saw me.

"Hey, Cunt-vacs," he snarled, "go grab her tits."

I didn't have to look to know whom that vindictive lowlife was talking about. I didn't move a muscle.

Now he was in my face.

"Did you hear me, dog? I said, 'Grab her tits'!" Big John commanded, now pointing directly at Angel.

Again, I didn't budge.

"That's a demerit, asshole! Give me your book!"

I opened my dogging kit, took out the virtually unblemished note-book, and handed it to him.

"Give him a brick," Big John said to no DZO member in particular as he scribbled inside of it. One of the Delta members hopped to and stuffed a red "Nassau" brick in my backpack.

"Now," Big John continued, handing my book back to me, "go grab her tits."

Once more I stood fast.

Big John pulled my dogging book out of my hands and again wrote in it.

"Give him another brick!"

Again, a nearby frat brother obliged.

A crowd was starting to gather around this confrontation. I could see that Angel had stopped on the outer fringe of the commotion to see what was going on. She had no idea this was all about her.

"Dog, you are disobeying a direct order," Big John barked. "Go grab her tits now!"

I refused.

"Another brick!" he screamed as he scrawled.

I was starting to feel the weight.

Again and again, Big John ordered me to take action, but I refused, a demerit was added to the book, and another brick was put in my back-pack. Where the hell they got all those bricks from I still have no idea.

When my backpack was filled with nearly a dozen bricks, Big John changed his tactic.

"Cunt-vacs, you are gonna suffer for this," he growled at one of the other pledge masters standing nearby. "Laugher, order your dog to go grab that girl's tits!"

"You got it, One Punch," Kevin "Laugher" Laughlin said cackling. "Crack...go grab Angel Levitano's tits."

Crack looked at me apologetically, then...

"Yes, sir!" he responded and headed in Angel's direction.

I looked and saw that she was still standing on the outskirts watching. When Angel finally realized that she was the focus of this exchange, she turned and started to run. Crack, not wanting to get a demerit, plowed through the crowd after her.

That's when I broke.

Despite the weight of my backpack and the distinct possibility that I was going to be blackballed for my actions, I ran after my fellow pledge and caught up to him just as he was about to grab Angel. I dove onto Crack and with the help of the additional weight on my pack and brought the big guy to the ground.

Angel turned and saw what I had done just as a horde of DZO members descended upon me. Her opinion of me was changed forever.

"You're a dead man, Cunt-vacs," Big John said with a certain amount of glee. "KICK HIS ASS!"

And they did.

* * *

As expected, my refusal to obey a direct order from my pledge master was brought up at the next meeting. Much to Big John's frustration and disappointment, I was not blackballed. For the most part, my refusal to obey had garnered even more admiration from Tank and my future Delta brothers. They saw me as a man of integrity, willing to stand up for what I believed in at any cost. Just the kind of pledge Delta Zeta Theta wanted. That doesn't mean I was exempt from punishment. As the rules of dogging dictated, I was still owed one paddle for every demerit...and Big John took his hatred for me out with every shot.

This was the last meeting before my Hell Night—the grand finale to the dogging period. After the meeting, the other pledges and I walked home together. Actually, after the beating Big John gave me, my walk was again more of a limp.

We shared the insanities of what our pledge masters had been putting us through and talked about what might happen to us at the coming Hell Night. We'd all heard tales of how other pledges before us had suffered and figured a lot of what we'd get would be much of the same. But we also knew there would be some surprises. Each year the current senior frat members tried to come up with some sick, original torment —most of which have been deemed inhuman by the United Nations —to outdo the Hell Nights of years before; a way for the graduating members to leave both a physical and metaphorical mark. None of us had any doubt that our guys had some truly fucked up things in store.

As we walked, one by one each of the group peeled off when we got to their neighborhood. Eventually, I was alone limping the final blocks to my house. Despite my aching ass, back, and thighs—Big John's aim was definitely lacking—I was feeling pretty good until I turned the corner onto my block and saw Jimmy O leaning against his car smoking a cigarette with one leather gloved hand while thrumming his fingers on the roof of his car with the other.

"Robert Kovac, Jr.," he said calmly, without even looking at me.

It was as if he knew the exact moment our paths would cross. Jimmy O was alone, and if I had to, I knew I could take him, but he didn't strike me as the kind of guy who fought fair. I said nothing but stood ready.

"You think joining Black and Green will protect you from me?" Jimmy O continued. "No. They may keep you from me, but they will never stop me from getting even with you."

"For what?" I decided to join the conversation.

"I have a reputation, Robbie," Jimmy O said, ignoring my question. "You made me look bad, so I need to settle the score. I won't stop until I do."

"I was saving my friend," I said, trying to reason with him.

Jimmy O's lack of aggression was definitely making me uncomfortable.

"You won't know where, when, or how, but someday, someway, I'll pay you back," he continued, again completely ignoring me.

"So why don't we settle this right now?" I said without any real conviction. I'd just been beaten up by my own frat. The last thing I wanted to do was fight.

"Good luck with your Hell Night, Bob," Jimmy O said ominously, taking one last long drag of his cigarette and shooting the still glowing butt off his fingers and into the street as he climbed back into his Camaro.

How did he time those things so perfectly?

He started his car and drove slowly away with the low rumble of glass pack mufflers providing the soundtrack.

I stood for a moment on high alert, listening as he drove off into the distance. When I was sure he was *gone gone*, I began limping the rest of the way home. If I lacked any motivation to finish my Delta pledging, I had it now. Even though, in my experience, guys like Jimmy O were all talk, no real action.

If only.

CHAPTER TEN

I have already mentioned those moments of clarity in our lives, and my Hell Night—all these years later—is still crystal clear, almost surreal in my mind. It was the weekend before Election Day and Richard Nixon—still years from the shame of his resignation —was running against youth favorite George McGovern. Being the first election where 18-year-olds were allowed to vote, the election of McGovern would have meant the immediate end of U.S. involvement in the Vietnam War. This was something I had a vested interest in as I was turning 18 in the spring and would be eligible for the draft. Yet I could not have cared less. All I was able to think about was what horrors might be in store for me as I tried to mentally and physically prepare for the long night ahead.

My parents were glued to the television, watching the big debate, as I got ready to leave the house.

"Where do you think you're going?" my dad asked, not really wanting an answer.

I knew what he really meant.

"This debate is important, Bobby," my mother said. "The outcome of this election could affect your future."

"I know, Mom," I said, solely because my parents' comments demanded some kind of response.

"That damn McGovern better not win. We need to finish things up over there," my dad said.

My father served during the Korean War and had been "face-to-face with the Commies" or as close as one can get flying a fighter jet. Even though he was in "The Forgotten War," he still felt the afterglow of World War II and just couldn't see how different things actually were this time.

"I have to go out," I said. "It's my Hell Night."

"Oh, the end of your hazing for that fraternity," my dad said with odd fatherly pride.

He still had no idea how different the high school frat system was from the ones during his college days.

"Well, be careful and put on a heavier coat, it's getting cold out there," said my mom.

At this point, between my lying and my dad's admonishments, she had completely bought into the idea that my joining a high school fraternity was some idyllic all-American thing. Hearing the love, caring, and sincerity in her voice, I actually felt bad deceiving her. But I had to see it through.

"Okay, I will," I said. "Go, Nixon."

I really wasn't a Nixon fan; he was way too swarthy and sweaty for me to trust. But I figured it was the right thing to say as I grabbed my winter coat from the hall closet and went out the door into the night.

"Go Nixon," my dad responded absentmindedly. He was already reabsorbed back into the debate.

As it started, so it ended. All four Delta pledges, having survived our various dogging periods, were ordered to meet the rest of the frat at Big John's house. Of all the times I'd been there—usually in the evenings but sometimes during the day—I had not once seen any of his other family members. I started to wonder if the wild animal was living on his own.

When I arrived, I found the streets packed with more cars than I'd ever seen there before and the other three pledges, once again, standing in the driveway.

"You're late," Creeder said.

Of the four pledges, Mofo Creeder was closest to me in age. He, too, had avoided joining a fraternity until it became absolutely necessary for his high school survival. But that's his story to tell.

"I'm not late," I replied. "They said 8:30 sharp."

"Well, they were all here and down in that basement when I arrived at eight," Crack said. "And they are wasted."

"How do you know?" I asked.

"Are you fucking kidding? Listen!" Drummer practically shouted.

Everyone went quiet, and I quickly tuned into the roar coming from the basement. I'd been at meetings before, and they were always crazy, but this sounded positively riotous.

"That can't be good," I said, stating the obvious.

"Ya think?" Stefko responded.

Just then the backdoor to the house opened, and Tank stepped out.

"Gentlemen! So good to see you!" he said, way too cheerfully.

I'd never seen him act like that before.

"We are going to be taking you in one at a time to complete the final part of your initiations, okay?" Tank added.

He was actually being pleasant. Now I was sure we were in for it.

"Mark, why don't you come in first?" Tank said cheerfully.

The four of us looked at each other, more worried than ever and silently wishing Creeder luck.

"The rest of you, relax and try to keep warm. It's chilly out here," Tank said with what appeared to be genuine concern.

We were so dead.

Moments after the door closed, the howling from the basement began, and complete insanity ensued. We had no idea what was going on down there, but judging by the screaming and shouting, it was Armageddon. There was no way of telling what was happening to Creeder, but the "soundtrack" told the three of us he was literally going through hell. Then the counting began. Slowly, the crowd in the basement began to shout.

"ONE! TWO! THREE! FOUR!"

This could only mean that Mofo was getting paddled, and on and on it went.

"FIFTEEN! SIXTEEN! SEVENTEEN! EIGHTEEN!"

Eighteen shots, and still it continued.

"THIRTY-SIX! THIRTY-SEVEN! THIRTY-EIGHT! THIRTY-NINE!"

How many DZO chapter members were down there!?

When the paddling finally came to an end, the count was at 55. Fifty-five shots! The crowd from downstairs roared, and a moment later the backdoor opened again. It was Tank. This time he was a bit sweaty and slightly out of breath.

"Drummer," he huffed pleasantly. "Why don't you come inside?"

Again we looked at each other, this time silently praying for Stefko. That time I actually said a prayer.

The exact same soundtrack happened for Joey and then Crack—complete with 55 shots—as I waited nervously for my turn. They were saving me for last again. As I stood out there in the cold, for the first time since that interview night, I gave some deep thought to whether or not this was all worthwhile. Maybe I should just get out of there? But Jimmy O's fateful words followed by Big John's premonition rang over and over in my head.

"You won't know where, when, or how."

"You're gonna need some brothers."

So I stood my ground.

Finally, the backdoor opened. Tank stepped out into the night air. He was a wreck.

"Woo, it's hot down there," he said, trying and failing to comb his disheveled hair with his fingers. "This night air feels good."

Even though I had taken my mother's suggestion and was wearing a heavier coat, I was freezing. But I was still in no rush to get inside.

"It sounds pretty bad down there," I said, trying to stall by making conversation.

"Ya think?" Tank said. "It probably sounds worse than it actually is. C'mon in."

So much for stalling...

I followed Tank through the house, and it seemed oddly quiet in the basement. As we slowly walked down the steps, I could hear the creak of each one. Tank crested the bottom several steps ahead of me.

"Gentlemen, Robert Kovac, Jr.," he said formally. "Show him a good time!"

As I hit the bottom step, I had only a fraction of a second to assess the room. There had to be 40 drunk, stoned, sweaty, smelly DZO members crammed in there. And then I was off...

Oddly, the roaring that had been the only thing I had to connect the inside with the outside didn't even register with what was happening to me now. If I didn't know better, I would have said it all happened in relative silence.

First, I was "taken around the room." This is where each of the 40-plus members of DZO in attendance, one after the other, smacked or punched me. And they weren't playful hits and slaps; each fraternal brother gave me all he had. I barely had time to breathe as member after member pounded me and then pushed me onto the next guy. It was absolutely brutal. For the grand finale, Big John side-kicked me in the stomach, knocking the wind completely out of me. I toppled to the floor, gasping for air. But they weren't finished. Before I could even slightly recover, I was yanked to my feet.

"OPEN YOUR PANTS!" a voice yelled.

I was so dazed that I didn't respond. I wasn't trying to be difficult; I was just too out of it to react.

"I SAID, 'OPEN YOUR PANTS'!"

This time I knew who it was. Tank. He didn't sound pleasant anymore.

I reluctantly opened them, not because I expected any kind of deviant weirdness, but because I knew exactly what was going to happen next. The Bretts had told me chapter and verse about this part of Hell Night at the lunch table.

The second I got them open, the waistband of my underwear was yanked violently out on all sides and filled with whole eggs, syrup, honey, cornflakes, and whipped cream. I mean filled. I was then ordered to close my pants up, which I did the best I could, considering how much stuff they had put in there. A lot of the raw eggs broke in the process and started dripping down my legs along with the syrup, honey, and now-liquefying whipped cream. I remember thinking, *This feels awful*, a thought that would soon become a happy memory.

Suddenly, I was grabbed, bent over, and held firmly—solidly—by several guys. Then the paddling began…and the rest of the eggs broke.

Remember when I said that each graduating class tried to figure out a way to up the dogging ante, so to speak? Well, Tank, Big John, and the rest of them came up with a doozy. Gone was the wide, thick, paddle-like board of old. My pledge class was introduced to a whole new experience involving a sawed-in-half baseball bat. Lucky us.

When I say, "Sawed in half," I don't mean across the wood bat creating a short handle-like paddle. I mean the barrel of the bat had been table sawed lengthwise creating a narrow long flat surface: a full-length "half bat" with plenty of swinging power.

One by one, each Delta member took a swing at my ass and upper thighs, beating me mercilessly. The guys were holding me so tightly that my body would barely move, making sure I received the full impact of every shot. I thought that my bones were going to break.

While each frat member got one shot, the officers and the pledge master each got three. This brought the total to 55. By the time it was nearing the end, my body was numb—I was probably in shock—and I wasn't feeling anything. But then it was Big John's turn to deliver the final three shots...and he made sure I felt each one.

Big John knew that night would be the last time he would have me at his mercy, and things hadn't gone the way he had hoped at all during my pledge period. I had taken every stupid thing he had to offer, and the one time I had screwed up, and he was sure I'd be blackballed, I wasn't. Big John was pissed off and ready to step up his game.

Where for the first 52 shots the bat had been passed around swiftly and the punishment executed mercifully quick—if the word "mercifully" can be applied to this torturous experience in any way—Big John was milking his final three. And everyone in the room knew it was time for his retribution.

"Spread out!" Big John ordered, and somehow this packed room was able to create space for ol' One Punch to do his dirty work.

"Take him down to the end of the room and put him up against the wall!"

At this point, I couldn't walk so they dragged me by my arms to the requested destination.

"Bend him over and hold him tight! I don't want his body to give an inch!" Big John barked.

"Hold it! Hold it! Hold it!" Tank's voice thankfully interrupted the proceedings. "You can't do that!"

Finally...a compassionate voice of reason.

"Put a coat or something between his head and the wall, so we don't crack his skull," Tank finished.

That was it? Out of all the insanity going on, that was where he drew the line? Someone folded up a jacket to cushion my head and absorb the impact.

"Can I do this now?" Big John asked, noticeably annoyed by Tank's interference.

"Fire away, oh mighty pledge master!" Tank responded.

And fire away he did.

Backing up to the opposite end of the basement and taking full advantage of the alley-like space the other frat members had created for him, Big John administered the most brutal shots of all: Screamers. This is where the paddler gives the paddlee running, spinning shots, taking the force and velocity of the hits to a whole other level. The only thing keeping me upright at all upon impact was the guys holding me rock steady.

"FIFTY-THREE! FIFTY-FOUR...!" The entire room chanted as Big John finished the job.

Believe it or not, there were rules to paddling. Go figure. I mentioned before there was no use of metal or sharp objects, but the cardinal rule —rule numero uno—was you never turn the paddle on its edge. This completely changes the physics of the paddle, and instead of the force being spread out over the entire surface, it is completely focused onto the very narrow area of the edge. On top of that, the paddle slices through the air with virtually no resistance. Now, with the new "bat paddle," there was technically no edge to speak up, but it still had a flat —albeit narrow—side that was, to some degree, less forceful than the corners…or the powerful rounded side of the bat.

As Big John spun across the basement floor for my final shot, at the last minute, he rolled the bat in his hands around to the business side and let me have it. The force and the pain literally knocked me unconscious. Unfortunately, that wasn't the last time a bat would turn out my lights.

When I finally came to, I was upstairs on the couch in the living room in extreme pain. I was surrounded by a swarm of green and black pulling at my clothes and doing something to my face. As my head began to clear, I realized they had stripped me down to my underwear and were dressing me in women's clothing while others were drawing on my face using waterproof marker pens. This was another part of the hazing ritual I had been warned about, but I couldn't believe that there wasn't some concern about my health considering my obvious condition.

"LET'S GO!" I heard Tank shout from somewhere.

Still in no condition to walk, I was quickly scooped up and dragged out the front door. The cold air felt great for a second, helping to clear my still-spinning head, but that clarity quickly grew to awareness. It was cold, and I was wearing stockings and a dress. Now what?

I didn't even have a chance to ponder the myriad possibilities before I was dropped onto the pavement and my brothers began to pour molasses all over me. Once I was covered, boxes of cornflakes and whipped cream quickly followed. This was the fraternity version of being tarred and feathered.

I wasn't the only one receiving this royal treatment. Each of the other three dogs got the same, and then we were each picked up and thrown into the trunks of cars. The final stage of Hell Night was about to begin.

The normal final challenge for pledges was to make their way back home after being dropped off together in essentially the middle of nowhere. Being locked in the trunk of a car for the duration of a joyride, then let out someplace potentially dangerous and without recognizable landmarks to orient them, the dogs had to finesse their way home without any money and looking like something out of a drag queen's worst nightmare. While they were driven around for hours to confuse them, the pledges were usually only taken 30-40 minutes away from home; and while cold, wet, tarred, feathered, and beaten, they could always make it back home safely. But I was "The Chosen One" and Big John was my pledge master. One Punch had darker plans for me.

As he drove away from the rest of the Hell Night terrorists, unbeknownst to me or Big John, for that matter, down the street, away from the center of activity, a car—with its headlights off—pulled out and followed a safe distance behind us.

Big John's disdain for me was beyond comprehension. All those weeks of me getting what he considered special treatment—on top of what I had done to him that first day of school—had pushed him to seek the ultimate revenge and do something that night that was unacceptable even by dirtbag fraternity standards. The goal of Hell Night was to hurt, harass, and make the pledges completely miserable, not to kill them. What Big John Russo did to me that night might have done just that.

While the other three pledge masters had stayed together on Long Island for their dog's final indignity—allowing the victims to at least have each other for support in finding their way home—Big John drove an hour and a half due north to upstate New York and brought me alone deep into the heart of the woods of Bear Mountain State Park. It may have only been a cold November night on Long Island, but it was near-freezing there. By the time Big John finally stopped the car, I was already half-frozen in the trunk. My teeth were chattering, my entire body was shivering, and my muscles had begun to lock up from the cold and the beating I had been given. Down the road, a safe distance from where Big John stopped, that same car that had followed

86

us from Long Island pulled over, again with its headlights off. I still had no idea it was even there.

Suddenly, the trunk popped open, and Big John looked in at me.

"Get out."

I literally couldn't move.

"I said, 'Get…'"

Big John violently dragged me out of the trunk and threw me to the ground.

"…the hell out!"

As I lay there in the dirt, Big John casually got back into his car, slammed the door, and started to drive away.

"Now you're fucked, Cunt-vacs!" he shouted from the open window as he sped off.

It began to lightly rain.

I lay there shaking, aching, and trying to gather my senses for several minutes, but then I forced myself to get up. I was in no condition to do anything, much less walk in the cold and dark; but I knew if I didn't start moving they would find me dead in the morning or whenever someone discovered my body. I had to find help. So with no idea where I was or any sense of direction, I began to stumble down the dirt road the way Big John's car had gone. I assumed he had headed toward the park exit. My legs screamed in pain, and the rest of my body was hurting, as well. I really was fucked.

Suddenly, a giant, hunched-over shadow splashed onto the road in front of me as a pair of bright car headlights flashed on behind me, and a V-8 engine roared into action. I turned and saw the car I didn't know had followed us as it jumped into action and sped toward me. Unable to move out of the way, my only thought was, *Jimmy O.* I was sure he had followed me all the way from Long Island to get even.

"You won't know where, when, or how."

Now, I was totally fucked.

The car screeched to a stop just a few feet in front of me, the door opened, and somebody leaped out.

"Get in!" the driver barked.

I was still blinded by the car's headlights and couldn't see.

"Who is it?" I asked, fearing the worst.

Then, from behind the lights and silhouette, I heard a familiar voice of salvation.

"It's me...Brett."

"Brett?" I managed to exhale...then I blacked out.

When I finally came to, I was in the back seat of a warm car with a blanket covering me—sticking to me was more like it. Brett was behind the wheel. Now that I had defrosted a bit, I was starting to think more clearly.

"You don't have a license," was the first thing I could think to say.

"Well, aren't you the observant one," Brett replied. "I don't have permission to use my parents' car either, but this didn't seem the time to play by the rules, did it?"

"But how—why did you follow us?" I asked.

"You're my friend; I didn't want you to be stranded," Brett said. "I just knew Big John was going to let you have it. There was no way he would just let you slide."

The full magnitude of what Brett had done for me—the chances he had taken—washed over me like the blessed heat coming out of the vents under the dashboard.

"Thank you," was the best I could say without getting overly emotional.

I could hear my dad's voice in my head as I fought back tears, *Big boys don't cry.*

"But where am I?" I continued once I had my emotions under control.

"Oh, Big John didn't lie…you were definitely fucked," Brett said. "He brought you to upstate New York and left you in the middle of a state park that's closed for the season. We're 65 miles from home!"

I didn't know what to say. My brain couldn't even fathom what I would have done if Brett hadn't saved my ass.

"There's a towel and some stuff back there to help you clean up and also a change of clothes," Brett said. "I knew mine would be too small so I borrowed some of my dad's."

"Your dad's?" I said a little too indignant.

"Hey, it's better than that Suzy Homemaker getup they dressed you in," Brett said. "Nice face, by the way. You're giving David Bowie a real run for his money."

I painfully lifted my head and body to look in the rearview mirror. They had done a real number on me with those waterproof markers.

"I'll never say anything about Bowie's makeup again," I said.

"You can't say anything about anybody's makeup again," Brett countered.

We drove awhile in relaxed silence. Even though it was the middle of the night and traffic was incredibly light, Brett still drove like a kid with a permit—which he was—sitting perfectly upright, hands at "ten and two" on the steering wheel, and making regular mechanical checks of his rear and side-view mirrors. I guess it would have sucked if he saved me only to get us killed on the drive home.

I cleaned up as best I could and changed into the clothes he had brought. I could see my legs and thighs were already badly swollen and turning purple and blue as I dressed.

"I'm sorry I haven't been around much lately," I finally said. "It's just this stupid dogging…"

"It's okay," Brett cut me off. "I get it. Besides, now my best friend is in Delta Zeta Theta. I'm a made man."

He was right. With all of the craziness, I had forgotten. I did it. I survived. I was now an official member of Black and Green.

"Wait...why do you need to be a made man?" I asked. "I was there for you before."

"Sure you were," Brett responded with a smirk, "but what if you just got lucky that day? Now I'm really protected."

"You're such a dick," I said.

"Maybe, but I saw yours under that dress you were wearing," Brett said. "Can't say I was impressed."

"Hey, it was cold outside!" I said with false indignity. "And why the hell were you looking under my dress?"

And we laughed. It literally hurt to do it, but it felt so good.

Brett was a real friend, a true friend. What he did for me that night —the chance he took—was something I would never forget. Brett was the kind of friend I'd never had before and would never have again.

* * *

"I call bullshit," interrupted Alex, breaking my flow and stopping the story in its tracks. "No one could survive that kind of physical abuse."

"Really, Robert, it's like something out of *Lord of the Flies*," Marie added pretty accurately.

"Why didn't one of you just call the cops?" Tommy asked.

Before I could open my mouth to answer, James stepped in.

"Because guys don't do that," he said. "Nobody put a gun to Robert's head to join that frat."

Well, maybe not technically, but it sure did feel like it. James was still close enough to high school and college age to remember what it was like.

"Yeah, I guess," conceded Tommy. "No one wants to be a pussy."

"Seriously?" said Marie, completely perplexed. "Men," she added, shaking her head.

"I still call bullshit," repeated Alex.

"Duly noted, Alex," said James. "Keep going, Robert...."

* * *

Hell Night was on a Friday, so I had the weekend to recover. I slept so long on Saturday that my mom started to worry and finally woke me up.

"Oh my God, Bobby!" she said, reacting to my overall look and condition. "Are you coming down with something?"

"Coming down with something was every mom's all-encompassing phrase for anything from being tired to cancer. Those four words strike terror in the hearts of mothers throughout the world. If one mom tells another that they think a family member might be coming down with something, the receiving mom—knowing the seriousness of the statement—will have sympathy anxiety in solidarity. My mom was ready to call a doctor.

Not wanting her to know the truth of my condition, I quickly put on my best game face and forced a Bobby-like grin.

"Jeez, Mom, can't a guy get a little extra shuteye without you calling the morgue?" I answered. As horrible as I felt, calling the county town morgue might not have been such a bad idea.

"I'll get you some baby aspirin," she said as she left the room.

Bayer, orange-flavored baby aspirin, was every concerned mother's cure-all. You would start being given them for pain or discomfort when you were an infant and, rather than switch you to regular aspirin, they would just increase the dosage as you got older. In my final year of high school, I was taking eight at a shot; what I really needed was a morphine drip.

If my mom had pulled back those covers, she would have screamed in horror. Hell, I almost did when I tried to get up to go to the bathroom; my legs were completely black, purple, and blue, and beyond swollen. My body had totally locked up, and when I tried to move, the blazing pain I felt matched how bad my legs looked. I bit my tongue and didn't make a sound for fear of my mother running back upstairs and seeing my true physical condition. She would have made me eat the entire bottle of baby aspirin on the way to the hospital.

A little while later Brett came over and helped continue the ruse with my parents. He made enough noise in my bedroom for both of us, giving my parents the illusion of normalcy. But in between loud wise-cracks and general stupidity, Brett let me know just how bad I looked. As if I needed his opinion.

"Oh man, what did they use on you, a bat?" he asked, literally hitting the nail on the head. "How the hell are you going to get a pair of pants over those things?"

He was right, my legs and butt were so badly swollen that a pair of harem pants would have been a tight fit. Once again, it was Brett to the rescue. He proceeded to make a series of clandestine trips down to the kitchen returning each time with either towels filled with ice or bags of frozen vegetables for me to put on my legs and butt to bring the swelling down. Even my little sister—who was way too smart to fall for that "I'm sleeping in" garbage—helped with the cold compress hustle Brett and I had going, running interference when either my mom or dad were getting too close to discovering the truth.

"Hey, Mom, can you help me with my homework?"

"Hey, Dad, did you really fly planes in the Korean War?"

Suzy was turning into a pretty cool kid.

At one point, Brett had to run to his house for fresh frozen supplies because I had used up all the ice and melted all the frozen food at mine. Thank God my parents didn't want a cold drink that day.

Sunday was a continuation of the treatment plan that started on Saturday, only the pain was even worse than the day before. I was sure I was going to have to "be sick" and miss school on Monday, even though it was the absolute last thing I wanted. I had earned my victory lap, and I was going to take it if it killed me. And I did.

CHAPTER ELEVEN

C ome Monday morning the two days of icing had its desired effect, and the swelling was down considerably. I still needed to wear my baggiest pants, but at least I could put on a pair. And the walking pain was manageable, albeit with a lot of baby aspirin in my system. But at least I could walk to school…and I did it in style.

In anticipation of making it through my hazing and surviving Hell Night, I had ordered and received my Delta Zeta Theta frat jacket in advance of actually completing my trial. I knew I had to make it to the end for reasons I've already stated. If I didn't, besides getting my ass kicked by Gamma Nu, I would have been out a cool $35—not chump change in 1972 dollars. I didn't dare try it on until that morning for fear that I would jinx myself. But I did pass the test, and as I left the house, I slipped on my DZO colors for the first time. *And damn, did they look cool.*

When I met up with Brett for our walk to school, he of course gave the appropriate huge reaction.

"Holy shit, you look amazing! Wait…what's purple and blue on the bottom, and Black and Green on top?"

Brett didn't wait for me to answer.

"You without your pants!"

True.

But what I had gone through—and was still healing from—didn't matter. I don't know when I've ever felt as good as I felt wearing those hard-fought colors that day. It seemed like everyone was checking me out admiringly. And even if they weren't, that's how I felt.

When Brett and I walked into The Commons area, there was no question that people were reacting. Pledging Delta was a huge deal in Baldwin High School, and because the whole dogging thing was so in everybody's face, you couldn't not know who was pledging for what fraternity. Everyone noticed I was wearing my colors and knew exactly what that meant. This said, the fact that I had been wearing red suspenders and a green bowtie for the previous two weeks definitely helped. Anyone who passed me, whether they knew me or not, shook my hand or at least gave me a smile or an admiring nod.

My frat brothers and sisters welcomed me into the fold with open arms, too…and with punches, smacks, and kicks in the ass. I said I didn't feel much pain walking. I didn't say I felt no pain. Each deliberate, targeted friendly hit was an instant reminder that I still had a lot of healing to go. They may have been literally busting my ass, but it didn't matter to me; I was bitchin'. Suddenly…

"Hey, Cunt-vacs!" Big John's loud dumb voice came from behind me.

As I turned to look at him, his right leg was already swinging with force toward my backside. And I knew that he wasn't going to give me a love tap. I quickly took evasive action and, using his own momentum against him and my right hand, I swept his leg up throwing him completely off balance and causing him to crash onto his back. His fat head bounced off the terrazzo floor.

For a second Big John was so stunned, he wasn't sure what had happened; his world had quickly been turned literally upside down. But then he roared back to life.

"CUNT-VACS!" he screamed as he started to get up.

I quickly slammed my foot forcefully onto his chest, knocking him back down; his head hit the floor for a second time.

"Never again," I said quietly yet forcefully. "You don't touch me ever again."

Big John lay on the floor and looked up at me, not even trying to get up. His big stupid brain was processing and registering the reality of what had happened. He knew that there was no way I had accidentally put him down three times. At that point, the entire school knew. I couldn't believe it took Big John that long to catch on.

"And another thing…," I heard Tank chiming in from nearby.

He stepped up and bent down to help Big John. I released my foot pressure from the idiot's chest as Tank pulled him to his feet.

"His name isn't Cunt-vacs," he continued.

Thank God, I thought to myself. *Any nickname is better than that.*

"Bobby's Delta name is New Guy," Tank finished with a smirk.

Did I mention that nicknames are rarely wanted or flattering?

One of the perks of being in DZO was getting to hang with the frat in The Commons and lunchroom. In fact, you were expected to hang with your fraternity brothers. Every time I wandered over to The Bretts' table, someone from Delta would call me back over to join them. It definitely felt like they didn't want me associating with people they thought were uncool, but it wasn't going to stop me; they were my real friends. Still, the mandatory associating with my frat brothers was going to mean less time for Brett and me, but as always, he understood. The fact that all the DZO guys and Theta girls now knew who he was and acknowledged him hadn't hurt his status either. And Aimee —Delta girl of flowery writing on cast—was even showing interest in dating Brent. As he said, Brent was a made man.

I was feeling more than a little mad myself, so when Angel Levitano floated through the lunchroom that day, I decided to finally make my move. I mean, how could she say no to a member of Delta Zeta Theta?

I rolled up on her wearing my DZO jacket and hit her with this gem:

"Hey...wanna go out with a member of Delta?"

Lame.

"No, thank you," Angel said curtly and kept walking.

What? I couldn't stop now, I had committed.

"No?" I said, driving the arrow deeper into my own heart. "But why not?"

"Because I won't date a guy in a gang," Angel fired back like it was something I should have already known.

"A guy in a gang?" I repeated, clearly remembering my using pretty much the same words the first time that I learned about them. "Well, who do you go out with?"

I could hear my mother's voice in my head going, "It's not who, it's whom!" There was no going back now.

Angel stopped suddenly and twirled around to face me for the first time. I didn't know what to make of this new turn of events, but she didn't look particularly pleased.

"I go out with nice guys who go out of their way to defend others, that's whom," she said, hitting the 'm' in whom hard.

Nice guys who defend others? Wait...

"But that's me," I said out loud, almost in disbelief.

"That's right," Angel said softly. "Come to my house this Sunday around five."

"Isn't that kind of early for a date?" I asked, stunned that she was asking me out.

I couldn't believe I was questioning her invitation, but the complete 180 the conversation had taken in mere seconds confused me.

"It's 'Sauce Sunday'; my whole family will be there," she answered. "You'll meet them, have something to eat, and then we'll go out after...if they approve."

"Meet your family?" Now I was really confused. "But I don't know where you live."

For some insane reason, I kept throwing up roadblocks.

Angel pulled out a pen, grabbed my hand, and started writing on it.

"If you don't meet my family, you can't take me out," she said like it was obvious. "But leave that jacket home; my parents won't let me go out with a gang member. And do not mention anything about your fraternity."

With that, she released my hand, turned, and walked away without looking back, but I was still talking.

"But I'm not...a gang...." I trailed off.

The whole encounter was so back and forth, on and off, it took me a second to absorb what had just happened. I looked down at my hand and read what Angel had written:

"1332 Shore Rd. 5 pm. No colors!"

And then it hit me...I had a date with Angel Levitano!!

* * *

Sauce Sunday—whatever that was—couldn't have come soon enough, but the long week gave me plenty of time to heal up from Hell Night and enjoy a pretty quiet week of fraternity life. Well, at least compared to my dogging and Hell Night.

I made one other frat connection of note that first week in Delta: with the only black member, Carl.

I was walking down the hall when he approached me. I already knew him from the frat meetings; he had dogged me and given me shots during my pledging weeks, but we had never really spoken.

"Hey, New Kid, you're not Jewish," he said.

"No?" I answered, sounding oddly unsure of my own religious upbringing.

It was a strange thing for someone to walk up to you and say.

"Why?" I asked.

"One of the guys in BLR told me that you said you are," he replied. "Did they tell you that you couldn't pledge Blue and Gold because you were Jewish?"

"Yup," I said.

"So, are you or aren't you?" Carl continued his cross-examination.

"Definitely not," I answered, clearing up any lingering confusion there might still be.

"So why did you tell them you were?" Carl asked.

"Because I didn't want to give them the pleasure of my denying it."

"Nice," Carl said with a laugh. "They did the same thing to me."

"You're Jewish?" I shot back.

Now we both laughed. This was quickly becoming an Abbott and Costello "Who's on first?" routine.

"They didn't actually tell you that you couldn't join because you're black, did they?" I continued.

"You bet your ass they did," Carl said. "And I didn't even ask to pledge their frat. Racist pieces of shit."

"Well, I would have told them I was black, too, but I didn't think I could pull it off," I said.

Carl laughed.

"What?" I continued, acting mock hurt as we walked off down the hall. "Are you denying me my heritage?"

Then we both laughed.

While I would be forever known in high school as New Kid, it could have been worse. Carl had a nickname, too. It followed his real name and was always implied, but never said: Carl... "The Black Kid." Sadly, it was how everybody knew him.

CHAPTER TWELVE

L iving on Long Island, having a driver's license was and still is an absolute necessity. As in any suburban or rural area where everything is completely spread out, other than by foot or by bicycle, you are extremely limited as to where you can go and what you can do. Dating is practically on hold from the age of 15 until you can drive. How can you seriously ask any girl out when you're "hoofing" it?

But driving means more than geographical freedom. It gives you your first taste of independence, as well, especially when you've got your own set of wheels. Your car becomes your first rolling apartment, albeit a very small one. But that little space is yours and yours alone, and for the first time in your life, you are truly free of your parents' total control. When I finally got my own car and things at home got to be a bit much to deal with, I would get in my car, drive around the block, park it, and just sit there listening to my music (on an 8-track tape player, of course) and reading my comic books, even if it were the dead of winter. In that case, I would run my heater as high as I wanted without fear of my father yelling at me for "wasting money." I was the king of Bobby's world, and nobody could tell me what to do. Long live the King!

* * *

I had only just passed my driver's test, and my parents kindly lent me their car for my big night out with Angel. Getting into DZO was what gave me the nerve to ask her out—although a non-starter with her—but being able to drive was the underlying key to my being able to make a move. And that Sunday at five o'clock sharp I knocked on the door of the Levitano house sans DZO jacket or any other sign of fraternity membership. The truth is that there were days I looked like a Black and Green idiot between my jacket, t-shirt, and a pair of Black and Green socks I had found in a store, but not today. I was dressed to impress for what I hoped would be the first of many dates with Angel Levitano.

The door opened, and there stood a boy, probably around 10 years old. He took one look at me, shook his head in disbelief, then…

"Angel," he called out, way too annoyed for someone his age. "Your boyfriend is here."

He said the word boyfriend like it meant victim.

Within seconds Angel was at the door, glowing as she always did. The kid stood his ground like he was her bodyguard.

"Thanks, Tommy," she said to what must have been her younger brother. "I've got this."

Tommy didn't move a muscle.

"Hey, Bobby," she said in the most neutral way possible.

She was giving me nothing to go on as far as her feelings about me being there.

"He's not that bad, Ang," Tommy said, looking me up and down like I was not such a prize steer.

Not that bad? What did that even mean?

"Tommy…go," Angel said firmly.

This time—with one last roll of his eyes—he did.

"Cute kid," I offered.

"Do you really think so?" Angel said in disbelief. "He's so annoying."

Yup, that was her little brother.

"Come on in," she continued, opening the door wider. "My family is waiting to meet you."

And they were.

Angel's family was Italian, and like so many who emigrated from other countries, when they arrived on these American shores they tended to stick with their own. Entire neighborhoods would grow around the culture of the "old country." "Little Russia," "Chinatown," and "Little Italy" are just a few of the many communities in the New York area that popped up and thrived. Visiting any of these areas on the outskirts of Manhattan was and still can be like a trip back to the old country, with the possible exception of an elevated train or two roaring overhead every few minutes.

As the years went by, these transplanted people got married, had families, and their families had families of their own. More times than not, those extended families continued to live in the same neighborhood— if not the same house—and a social clan was born.

For Italians, getting everyone together once a week for a meal was an old country tradition that they continued in the new country. Every Sauce Sunday, the entire extended family would descend upon the senior family member's place of residence—or the relative with the biggest house—and everyone would join in preparing a feast.

When Angel had told me that I would be meeting her family, I assumed she meant her mother and father and maybe her bratty little brother, Tommy. The equivalent of what she would have met if she had come to my house. I had no idea that she meant every single relative she had.

The house was alive with activity, packed with people young and old.

"You look nice," Angel said to me under her breath, sounding almost relieved. "Are you ready?"

"For what?" I started to answer, but she was already ushering me along. First stop: The Formal Dining Room.

Walking into that room was like entering the set of *The Godfather*. The movie had only recently come out, and when I saw it, I assumed that the familial atmosphere depicted on the screen was a Hollywood creation. Nope. Francis Ford Coppola's portrayal of Italian family life was spot on. I could have sworn I heard "The Godfather Theme" playing softly in the background when I entered the room. There's a pretty good chance that it was. The massive table in the formal dining room seated at least 14 with a few extra chairs pulled up to accommodate the overflow. If this was the set of *The Godfather*, Angel's family was most definitely from Central Casting.

Grandparents, aunts, uncles, her parents—every adult member of the family—were packed in there. I didn't know if this gathering was a weekly affair or just to meet me, but all eyes locked on yours truly when Angel and I entered. Everybody was smoking and drinking coffee, and for a moment it seemed that all motion—including the floating cigarette smoke—froze.

"Everybody, this is Bobby Kovac, the boy I was telling you about," Angel announced.

"H-hi?" I said, suddenly nervous.

Why was that a question?

Everyone in the room simultaneously greeted me in various formal ways. I'm pretty sure the grandparents were speaking Italian.

"Introduce him to your cousins," a very large, intimidating man at the head of the table finally said.

"Yes, Daddy," Angel replied.

My God, that bear was her father.

She proceeded to lead me out of the dining room and into the kitchen. It was filled with younger people sitting and standing around the dinette.

"Everybody, this is Bobby," Angel again announced. "Bobby, this is my sister Lisa Marie, my cousins, and my brother Tommy whom you already met."

There were a lot of cousins; I totally understood why she didn't bother naming each one.

The response from this bunch was a lot friendlier and more upbeat. I was offered a seat, and something to drink, and then I answered a series of questions as quickly as they were fired off.

"Are you Italian?"

"No."

"Half-Italian?"

"No."

"Maybe just a little Italian?

"I don't think so."

My last answer that they pressured out of me apparently gave the slightest chance that I might be wrong about my own cultural background. My use of the word "think" suggested—at least as far as they were concerned—that there was a possibility someone in my family's lineage had enjoyed the intimate company of a person of Italian descent, so that line of questioning came to an end.

"Where are you from?"

"Ohio."

"Do you have your own car?"

"I'm getting one."

At this point Angel, like me, had had enough.

"I'll be right back," she said with a smile that read, "I'm getting out of here." Then she left the room.

Throughout the grilling, one cousin had sat silent. She was the oldest —probably in her twenties—pretty, and she definitely looked more "worldly." I'm being as PC as possible here.

"You're a pretty good-lookin' guy," she said, checking me over like I was a prize bull. "What are you doing with Angel?"

I was stunned to hear something that blunt spill out of the mouth of a family member. Later I would discover why.

This was Cousin Francine. Everyone called her "Frankie," but among the family, she was known as "La Puttana," Italian for "The Slut." Before she disappointed the family with her life choices, Frankie had always been considered "the pretty one" as in, "She's pretty but not as beautiful as Frankie." Angel, on the other hand, had been known as The Ugly Duckling. An awful thing to call any child, but knowing the children's story behind that name and Angel's end result, it actually seemed more like a prophecy.

Frankie may have seen the writing on the wall as she and other family members shared the terrible name-calling of her classmates. She particularly reveled in the Flatsy Patsy designation. Family can be just as mean as the outside world.

I was processing my answer to Frankie's backhanded compliment and insult to the woman of my dreams...when one of the aunts entered the kitchen.

"The family will see you now," she said to me very formally.

The family? I thought I had just met them.

"Have fun," Frankie said with a smirk.

I'm guessing many of her suitors had been to the Sauce Sunday dance.

I stood up and followed the aunt out of the room. Angel hadn't yet returned from wherever she had gone, so it appeared that I was going it alone.

This time when I entered, the atmosphere was a bit lighter. There was an open chair for me at the end of the table directly opposite her father with the rest of the adults lining either side like a jury. As I said, it was only a bit lighter. As with the cousins in the kitchen, the elders began to ask me a series of small talk questions, which I answered as quickly and politely as I could. As a rule, I did really well with parents.

"Are you Italian?"

What was it with those people?

"No."

Disapproving glances all around.

"Are you maybe a little Italian?"

They cut to the chase.

"I don't think so."

This worked with the kitchen crowd, and it seemed to satisfy this bunch, too. They all nodded to one another silently saying, "There's hope."

"Nice weather we're having, isn't it."

It had actually been kind of cold, but I wasn't going to throw any negativity into the conversation.

"Yes, it has been lovely."

I was really pouring it on.

"What does your father do for a living?"

"He's a retired sergeant major for the United States Air Force now working at Grumman Aerospace doing aircraft research and development."

This wowed the crowd. A former officer with a steady job at Grumman; they were impressed.

"Vito imports olive oil," said an elderly woman with motherly pride, as she pets the hairy arm of the bear at the head of the table.

He imported olive oil? Seriously? That was the business the Corleone family in *The Godfather* was in. Everyone knew what "importing olive oil" meant.

As the line of innocuous, yet pointed questions continued about sports, the election—Angel's parents couldn't stand dirty hippies—and other topics of the day, it all felt oddly like the DZO grilling I got the night of my interview.

As the exchange continued, I couldn't help but notice the room was thinning. One by one, people were getting up and leaving until all that was left was Angel's father and four burly uncles, two on either side of him. If the full table was the jury, then this was definitely the firing squad. I was just finishing up an answer to one of their questions…

"And once I graduate college, I'm hoping to get a job in—"

"All right, enough with the bullshit," Angel's father growled at me.

What bullshit? I really did plan on going to college.

"What do you want with my daughter?" he finished.

If ever there was a loaded question, that was it. What did I want with a beautiful 17-year-old girl? I was a teenage boy! My mind raced for a more acceptable answer.

"Well, sir, Angel is an amazing young woman, and I'd really like to get to know her better," I stammered. "Who knows, maybe our relationship will develop into something meaning—"

"Cut the bullshit," the bear said.

Again with bullshit?

Now all five of them were staring straight at me, their eyes dark and unblinking. It was like looking down the barrels of 10 guns.

"Bobby, there are two kinds of problems in this world: gun problems and bat problems," Angel's father continued conversationally. "Baseball bat problems are things that require action to be taken, but they don't need a permanent solution. You know, little problems."

I was glad for the clarification. For a second there, I actually thought he was talking about flying bats.

"Now gun problems, those are problems that need a more permanent solution," he went on. "Like, say, if you were to hurt my Angel—in any way at all—I would consider that a gun problem."

This was the man who didn't want his daughter associated with fraternities because he thought they were gangs?

Then came his big finish.

"If you lay one hand on my daughter, this family will hunt you down to the four corners of the earth and put you in the bottom of a lake. Do you understand?"

Right then and there, at that moment—as my brain was screaming, "Kovac, get out of this house now!"—my heart told me something that I probably already knew: Angel was the one. I would do and deal with anything to win this girl's heart, and nothing would ever stop me. I wasn't going anywhere.

"Yes, sir, I understand," I said. "I will never hurt your daughter."

And I meant it.

"Good," Angel's father said with a nod and a bit of a smile. "Then we have no problem."

As on cue, Angel's mom, grandparents, and aunts drifted back into the room. They had to have been eavesdropping.

"Did you boys have a nice talk?" Angel's mother asked.

"Very nice," her dad answered buoyantly. "Bobby's taking Angel out on a date tonight.

I made it!

The connection between Angel and me was immediate and strong. On that first date, we talked for hours and quickly came to know each other, establishing the framework for a relationship that could last a lifetime. Angel was smart—in all advanced classes—and talented—a choir and drama club member. She couldn't care less about hanging out with the "in crowd." Her goal was to graduate with honors and attend an Ivy League school.

Angel liked me for all the right reasons; for the person I was, not the frat boy I was trying to be. Just being with her made me a better person; I knew that with her was where I had to be. But the demands of being in DZO were a fly in the ointment of our relationship. Something that I initially had zero interest in being involved with—and only joined for self-protection—had oddly become the focal point of my life.

"I've watched you, Bobby Kovac," Angel said. "You're a good guy."

I knew there had to be a "but" in there somewhere.

"But…" she continued.

There it was. My father had always said everything before the word "but" was bullshit.

"…when you're around that fraternity, you act like a different person."

I tried to explain that I wasn't acting like or trying to be anything. The Bobby she liked was who I was, but she would have none of it.

"I think the fraternities are made up of arrogant, obnoxious idiots who believe high school life revolves around their stupidity."

Ouch.

"I'm not saying that you have to quit," she continued. "I just want to go out with the real Bobby Kovac."

While Angel was pretty much on the nose with her assessment of the frats, I didn't totally agree with her. As I had learned that night walking home from my interview, there was definitely a brotherhood among the DZO members; they had each other's back, and I definitely needed that. The ongoing Jimmy O problem had only quieted because I was dogging for and now in Delta. I had come to believe that a fraternity was something worth being a part of, but the last thing I was going to do was fight with her about it. Angel Levitano was willing to go out with me, and that was all I cared about. I wanted her to share everything with me, but if leaving her out of my DZO life was the only way we could be together, I'd take what I could get.

When I look back on those times with Angel, all I remember is sunshine. I know it sounds stupid, but I can't remember a dreary or bad day. Of course, some days were cold, some days were hot, and on others, it rained or snowed, but I can't remember one day or night I spent with her that wasn't beautiful. That was the effect Angel Levitano had on me. Sometimes I couldn't even believe she was real. If the only reason Angel went out with me was that she thought I was a nice guy, I decided that I would do everything in my power to build on that. I believed that if I really tried, I could turn the like she had for me into love. I had already lost my heart to her, and I wanted Angel to feel the same way about me. To paraphrase Jack Nicholson's character in the movie *As Good As It Gets*, "She made me want to be a better man." When I was with her, I was thoughtful, courteous, charming, smart, funny, generous, and more. And it wasn't an act. It was the best me; the me Angel knew I was.

If only she had the same effect on me when I wasn't with her.

Like the separation of church and state, the idea of me having independent frat and personal lives was great in theory but turned out to be awful in execution.

CHAPTER THIRTEEN

The winter months brought a lot of fraternity "brew-ups." These were weekly parties held at various frat members' houses—whoever's parents were out or gone for the weekend, usually Big John's—with a lot of drinking and pot smoking. These gatherings usually got too rowdy and ended up in drunken/stoned behavior and fighting. The fighting was not so much between DZO members—though that happened often enough—but with other fraternities who tried to crash the parties or with other frat members the Delta guys found when they went cruising around looking for trouble after the brew-ups. I initially resisted going to these gatherings at all but quickly found out that if you were in Delta Zeta Theta and wanted to stay in Delta Zeta Theta, you'd damn well better show up at these gatherings. At first, I tried to avoid over-drinking and partying and steer clear of the wanton violence. But slowly, inexorably, I found myself pulled into the lifestyle, indulging more and more. It wasn't good.

The average brew-up was held on a Friday or Saturday night. Everybody would get there around eight o'clock, and the members who were old enough to buy beer would pick up a few cases on the way over; everybody was expected to chip in.

The minute the beer got there, the membership clamored for the cans and bottles like they had just walked out of the Sahara Desert and were dying of thirst.

There were usually 25 to 30 guys in attendance—no women allowed with the exception of the occasional girl or two who were willing and liked to party—so there was no dress code or social etiquette of any kind. All in all, it was just a bunch of testosterone-fueled teenage guys with raging hormones out to raise some hell and have a good time.

At the very first party I attended, I tried to avoid getting pulled into the debauchery.

"New Kid, here you go!" someone said, offering me a beer.

"Thanks, man; I'm good," I responded, trying to sound as matter-of-fact as possible.

"You won't share a drink with your fraternal brotherhood?" Tank asked suspiciously, and a little too loudly so everyone would hear.

All conversation ceased, and every eye in the room turned toward me. This was as dramatic a question as any presented during my DZO interview. There was only one acceptable answer, and I knew exactly what I had to say.

"Of course, I'll share a beer with my brothers, Tank. Let me have one!"

Still not a word was said, and no one took their eyes off me until I cracked open that can and took a good long swig. Only then did the party kick back into gear.

On most nights, after the beer came pot; and after the pot came the hard liquor. It was an impossibly slippery slope once you caved to having that first drink. But what were the choices? With DZO, you were either all in, or you were out. I still needed to be in. But of the women, I stood firm and did not partake.

Through it all, my Jekyll and Hyde relationship with Angel continued to grow. Well, at least my Dr. Jekyll side did. In school, we each did our own thing. Most days Angel had something to do after school with the drama club or choir, and I hung out with Brett or the guys in the frat. On the weekends, she and I would spend the night that there wasn't a Delta brew-up together, and every Sauce Sunday was spent with her family sans any evidence of fraternity membership.

Now, I knew I didn't have any Italian in me, but I thought I ate like one. The family even gave me a nickname, "The Gavone." I was so proud; it made me feel like a part of the clan. I thought that it meant "Good Eater" since it was always used in relation to how much food I could consume.

"Look at this guy; what a gavone!"

"Don't let it go to waste. Give it to The Gavone; he'll eat it."

It wasn't until I took a trip to Italy many years later that I found out gavone was Italian slang for the village idiot. So much for being accepted.

Things were working out pretty well as the end of the year and holidays approached; after a month of going out together, Angel and I were growing closer by the day. On top of that, as we headed into December, I had not seen hide nor hair of Jimmy O or anyone from Gamma Nu since before my Hell Night. It seemed like my DZO play had been the right move to make and my problem solved. If only...

CHAPTER FOURTEEN

I was at a DZO brew-up the first weekend in December when Black and White once again made its presence known. This time not just to me, but to my entire frat.

While we were all down in Big John's basement having our weekly good time, almost every one of our cars was vandalized by Gamma Nu: tires slashed, and windshields smashed. And right on the hood of Tank's mint 1970 Mustang GT fastback, someone literally took a shit. *A human shit.* These hostile actions predated the obligatory built-in car alarms of today—the ones nobody pays attention to when they go off. Back then, car alarms were an aftermarket affair and not something the average high school student could afford to have installed. Any money they did have was better spent on cool custom rims or a bitchin' car stereo. So as our vulnerable, silent cars were being desecrated outside, we Delta boys partied on in the basement. And just so there would be no confusion as to who was responsible for these hostile actions, the scumbags signed their work. On the side of each and every car in black and white spray paint were the Greek letters:

$$\Delta \Gamma N$$

Delta Gamma Nu.

This meant war.

Now you might be wondering what the deal was between the various fraternities within Baldwin High School itself; surely there must have been some friction and rivalry. The answer is simple: established hierarchy.

Within the school structure, each frat well knew its place in the pecking order. At the top—side-by-side—Delta Zeta Theta and Beta Lambda Rho stood tall. As both were comprised of varsity athletes who were used to playing on the same team, most of them were friends, so the two frats got along. With the big dogs standing staunchly together, the sheer numbers and influence they had made every other smaller club toe the line. Sure, there was the occasional scuffle and mix-up between individual members of the different clubs —Big John certainly had his fair share—but these were insignificant moments quickly smoothed over by the calmer heads of the club leaders. For the most part, the fraternities policed their own. Besides, they all had a much bigger fish to fry, namely Delta Gamma Nu. Black and White were an annoying thorn in the side of virtually every fraternity.

You see, while Gamma Nu hated DZO, we were not their only target. Black and White were in the business of conflict and mixed it up with any and every club without exception. They must have laid awake nights thinking up different ways of butting heads and instigating trouble with not only the fraternities in their own town but the ones in surrounding towns, as well. Plotting and planning this vast required a criminal mastermind, and his name was Jimmy O. Since taking control of the club in his first senior year, he had brought Gamma Nu's aggression and open hostility to new levels. This kept all the frats unified and focused on their common adversary: "my enemy's enemy is my friend."

Now, unlike military wars, fraternity conflicts like the one between DZO and Gamma Nu were organized events with an agreed date, time, and place of mutual choosing. Kind of like, "Meet me after school this afternoon behind the firehouse" but on a much grander scale. With the Christmas break fast approaching, the fight had to take place before the holidays when various members wouldn't be able to attend due to a variety of religious and familial obligations. Ridiculous I know, but it was high school. Communications between Gamma Nu and Delta were had, and the face-off was set: Saturday, December 15th, at 1 pm... Silver Lake Park.

Silver Lake Park sat square on the border of Baldwin and Oceanside between Merrick and Fox Hurst Roads. A small "walking" park without a playground of any kind, it would be desolate at that time of year. The perfect setting for a showdown.

While I didn't relish the idea of being involved in a rumble of this magnitude—it wreaked of Angel's dreaded "gang activity"—I was glad this was something the entire frat stood behind. For once, I wasn't being singled out as a target by Gamma Nu and needing protection from my frat; we all were in their sights. Still, Jimmy O did have a personal score to settle with me, so I was grateful to have my crew behind me.

Now, just like DZO had its friendly fraternal relationships, Black and White had its own partners in crime, as well. Clubs like Beta Kappa Phi and Black and Purple stood with their dirtbag brethren in a pinch; and in this coming war, people were definitely having to choose sides. And as the numbers involved grew, so did local awareness.

By the week of the battle, the number of combatants and frats partici- pating had grown to the point that discussions were being held to move the rumble to a bigger venue for fear that tiny Silver Lake Park couldn't accommodate the number of people expected to show up. This war would be of epic proportion. And that's when—to no one's surprise—word of the fight reached the Baldwin and Oceanside police precincts, and the event was forcibly shut down.

In order to calm the still-hostile fraternities, a call was put in by Ethel Kloberg to her dean of students counterpart at Oceanside High, Mr. Whittier. She requested that he ask the leaders of DGN if they would consider sitting down with DZO to settle this problem amicably. While Deans Kloberg and Whittier saw this meeting as peace talks, Gamma Nu and Delta saw it for what it really was: a war council.

Six members from each fraternity were invited to participate in the summit. For Delta, this meant our club president, Tank; vice-president, Frankie the Mouth; club treasurer, Jerry Strong; and our intrepid sergeant-at-arms and resident hothead, Big John Russo. That left two more members to attend.

"You're coming with us," Tank blurted out to me at lunch two days before the big meeting.

"Me? Why would you include me?" I asked, mystified by the command. "I've only been an active member for a month."

"You know how to handle yourself, you're the only one of us who has actually beaten Jimmy O in a fight, and you've got a lot riding on this whole Gamma Nu thing," Tank rattled off his answer like he knew the question was coming.

He wasn't wrong, and I couldn't honestly say I had no desire to be there. I did have a lot invested in the outcome of this event, even more than I realized.

* * *

"And why do you have to be there?" Angel asked after I told her about being invited.

"Because they think I can be of help," I answered, surprised by her question. "I consider it an honor to be asked."

"This is exactly the kind of thing I don't like about your involvement with these fraternities," she said.

"But they're peace talks," I added, trying to defend the indefensible.

"Peace talks?" Angel responded in disbelief. "You stupid fraternities were planning such a huge fight that the police had to step in, shut it down, and ask the schools to try and mediate things! That's not peace talks, that's a war council!"

How did she know? As always, Angel was right. But still...

On Friday, December 15th, a half dozen "members" of Black and White, led by Jimmy O, soldiered in through the side door of Baldwin High. Mr. Whittier, the diminutive Oceanside High dean of students trailed behind them desperately trying to keep up. Their entrance was made through the door closest to the intended meeting place—The Little Theater—directly adjacent to Dean Kloberg's office.

I put members in quotes because, other than Jimmy O, I had never seen a single one of those guys before; and I had run into quite a few of them. All five were physical monsters who looked—like Jimmy O— way too old to still be in high school. None of them were even wearing true Gamma Nu colors. One was wearing a cutoff Black and White t-shirt—in the winter—and another had cut the Old English lettered Delta Gamma Nu logo from the back of a frat jacket and roughly sewed it to his black motorcycle jacket; other than that, they were without colors. Gamma Nu arrived between classes, and the mere sight of them entering the building literally stopped hall traffic dead.

I was standing just outside the dean's office with my guys waiting for their arrival, and I clearly remember seeing all four of The Brets in the hall outside of the lunchroom staring at the Gamma Nu guys as they walked in. Their mouths were literally hanging open; not a poker face in the bunch.

Before the twelve of us could even lock eyes, the short but sturdy Dean Kloberg—a former Baldwin High women's gym teacher and coach— emerged from her office with Jimmy O-like timing to step between the two clubs. She must have gotten a call that they had arrived.

"Gentlemen," the dean started off, addressing Jimmy O and his crew —I could have sworn a couple of them actually looked around to see who she was talking to—"welcome to Baldwin Senior High School. Thank you for agreeing to come."

Quickly, before Jimmy O or any of his goons could respond, Dean Whittier scurried around to the front of his pack.

"Thank you, Dean Kloberg," he said very formally, "it is an honor to be invited to your house of academia."

"All right, let's not get carried away, Whittier," quipped Jimmy O.

His crew laughed, and most of us in DZO did, too. None of us had any misconception as to what this meeting really was.

The Little Theater was literally that. It had seats like a regular auditorium, but the number was maybe 75 with a small low stage—really more of a glorified platform, maybe two feet high—at the front. When we entered the room, Coach Landers and Mr. Medlock—Baldwin High's tough-as-nails, ex-Marine, Blackfoot Indian shop teacher—were waiting at the door to meet us, clearly for security reasons. They didn't seem too thrilled with their designation as glorified bouncers.

Coach Landers led our guys down the right aisle of the theater, and Mr. Medlock took Gamma Nu across the back and down the left side. When the procession reached the front, we all crossed the narrow space between the first row and the stage and sat down 10 across. Miss Kloberg and Mr. Whittier took their seats on the stage with Tank and Jimmy O sitting on either side of them.

Somehow, I wound up the first person from our side to enter the row. This sat me right next to the Gamma Nu gorilla with the cutoff Black and White t-shirt. On his forearm, he had a military tattoo.

"You're an Air Commando?" I asked in disbelief. "Impressive."

"What?" he responded, completely thrown by my recognition of the logo on his arm.

The Air Commandos is a special operations component of the United States Air Force that handles specialized airpower. Not just any airman can be an Air Commando. This bruiser was definitely no high school student.

I looked up at the stage just in time to catch Jimmy O hard staring at me. When he caught my eye he smirked, winked, then gave a slight nod. I knew exactly what he was saying.

"Gentlemen," again began Dean Kloberg, "the Baldwin and Oceanside precincts of the Nassau County Police Department have asked if we would arrange this meeting in an effort to cool the current hostilities between you."

"Current?" Tank inserted.

Again, both frats chuckled. It was nice that we could find humor as a common ground.

"This is anything but humorous," Dean Whittier quickly injected. "If the authorities hadn't stepped in, people could have been seriously injured. Not to mention the wanton destruction of personal property."

You could definitely tell that Dean Kloberg had been a coach and Whittier was a former English teacher.

"Well, none of this would have even gone down if DZO hadn't vandalized our cars," Jimmy said, way too casually.

All six of us from Black and White erupted.

"Vandalized your cars?!" Tank retorted in shock. "We didn't touch your stupid cars, but you completely fucked up ours!"

"Language!" Dean Whittier cried.

He apparently saw himself as the guardian of civility.

"You see what we have to deal with?" Jimmy O said to the two deans with mock innocence.

Thankfully, Miss Kloberg wasn't buying any of it.

"Mr. O'Reilly, I saw DZO's police report," she said. "There were thousands of dollars of damage done to their vehicles, and your fraternity's Greek letters were painted on all of the cars."

"I'm telling you, it wasn't us," Jimmy O proclaimed. "Look, all I know is our cars were wrecked, and DZO's letters were spray painted all over them."

Again, my guys erupted, but this time the Gamma Nu guys joined in feigning mock indignation over the made-up damage to their imaginary vehicles.

"Do you have your police report?" Dean Kloberg asked calmly.

Damn, that woman was cool.

"Nobody told me we were supposed to bring it," Jimmy O responded like some kid who had forgotten his homework.

"That is such a load of shit, and you know it asshole!" Tank barked across Kloberg and Whittier at Jimmy O.

"Language!" shouted Dean Whittier as the room once again erupted.

"Gamma Nu trashed our cars and started this war," Tank added, setting the record straight. "Delta is gonna fucking finish it!"

"Not if we finish you first," Jimmy O replied with true menace.

Tank and Jimmy O both stood up and went for each other.

Following their club president's lead, the frats leaped to their feet for some action, but the narrow space between the seats and the front of the stage left little room for movement. Both sides tried to get to the other but couldn't, only succeeding in shoving me and Mr. Cutoff T face-to-face.

"So you know what an Air Commando is?" he hissed quietly, somehow cutting through the commotion around us.

"Yeah, I do," I responded. "And you are a goddamn disgrace to the command."

That got him.

"FUCK YOU, KID!" he said way too defensively, shoving me back hard into my guys who were clamoring behind me.

Spoken like a true high school student.

And that was it. Both frats started climbing over and onto the low stage and chairs and throwing punches at each other. This brought

Coach Landers and Mr. Medlock out of the wings and into the fray as Tank and Jimmy O tried to engage in a shoving match. Impressively, Dean Kloberg had no problem keeping them apart.

When it was all over, besides a few bumps and bruises, Gamma Nu and DZO agreed to call off their feud. Of course, both Dean Kloberg and Whittier had to threaten the mass expulsion of both frats from their respective schools to help convince them to come to their senses. On top of that, the holidays were coming, so no one really had any motivation to continue hostilities...for now.

CHAPTER FIFTEEN

As I've mentioned, my parents are of Eastern European descent. People from that region are described with words like sturdy, gritty, and intense and are known best for suffering through and dealing with hardships and oppression. Not the most flowery descriptive. My family hadn't any direct experience with misery on that level, but these characteristics are part of our DNA, and my upbringing reflected it. There was nothing warm and cuddly about being a Kovac. Don't get me wrong; I'm not saying my childhood was an unhappy one. Up until meeting Angel, I thought my home life was great. But compared to the Levitanos, the Kovac's household was positively Spartan.

Now, the single word always used to describe Italians is "passionate." This quality permeated everything about them and was particularly evident around the holidays. My first Christmas with Angel and her family changed my life forever.

In my house, Christmas was always a very special time of year. It included all the usual stuff: decorations, a tree, holiday music, Christmas dinner, church on Christmas Eve, and getting and giving presents. Fun. Italians, however, took this holiday to a whole other level. From the decorating to the food to the gift-giving to Christmas mass itself, everything was amplified by the passion for being Italian. It was Christmas times 100.

Being this was to be my first Christmas with Angel, I really wanted to impress her. The gifts exchanged in my house were always practical, utilitarian, and rarely frivolous. Getting a present that you wanted "just because" was the exception, not the rule. That was not going to be the case with my Christmas gift for my new girlfriend.

Today a television in every room may be the norm for a lot of households, but in the '70s it was the exception, not the rule. Angel had mentioned in passing one day how she would really love to have her own TV, and I decided that this Christmas I would make that wish come true. So, I got a part-time job working for a local Christmas tree lot during the holidays to help pay for her gift.

Every year a tree farm owner from Vermont named Sage brought a tractor-trailer full of trees down to Long Island to sell during the holiday season. It was hard, sticky work and the days were long and cold; but for a gift as extravagant as a portable television, I had to put in a lot of hours. A 12" black and white portable went for about $100 back then—that's almost $600 in today's dollars. So I worked my ass off, earned the money, and bought a super expensive gift for my girl. I thought it would literally show Angel just how much she meant to me.

Christmas Eve finally arrived, and I loaded the huge, colorfully-wrapped box with a big bow on it into the trunk of my parents' car and headed to Angel's house. I was positive that my gift was going to blow her mind.

When I got there, the street was packed with cars. People from all over the neighborhood were heading to the Levitanos carrying food, alcohol, and gifts, drawn like moths to a flame by the over-the-top Christmas decorations on their house. It was so lit up for the holidays their electric bill must have looked like a mortgage payment. Oddly, the closer I got to Angel's house, the smaller my gift seemed to get. By the time I got inside and added it to the massive pile of presents already under and around the Christmas tree, mine looked like it was a perfume box.

On Christmas Eve, Italian-American Catholic families celebrated the Feast of the Seven Fishes. Apparently, only eating a boatload of fish was some kind of fast, saving the eating of massive amounts of red and other animal meat for Christmas Day. Whatever the reason, the food was abundant and incredible; the "Gavone" earned his name that night.

Having only been dating Angel for a couple of months, I wasn't expecting anything from her family for Christmas. Why should they have gotten me a gift? I still don't know the answer, but whatever their reasoning, Angel and the Levitanos buried me in presents. I mean I was covered. The wash of wrapping paper on the living room floor was literally knee-deep, and at one point, I merrily waded through it like a kid kicking a pile of raked leaves in the fall. It was positively surreal.

Now, if my present for Angel had felt small before the gift-giving, it seemed practically insignificant after the deluge that I received. I was almost ashamed to give it to her. But when Angel opened it, she made me feel like a hero. She couldn't believe I remembered what she had wanted and knew full well how much it cost and how hard I must have worked to afford it. You would have thought that I had buried her in presents, too. Even her mom and dad were impressed with my gift. And that's when Angel shocked me. From behind the Christmas tree, she pulled out one last wrapped box and took me into another room where we could open it alone.

"What's this?" I asked, not thinking for a second it had anything to do with me.

"It's for you," Angel answered.

"Seriously?" I said in disbelief. "Come on, Angel, you've given me way too much already."

"It's just a little something I made," she said dismissively. "It's no big deal."

I took the package from her hands and slowly opened it, not really knowing what to expect. It was a sweater...but not just any sweater. It was a hand-knitted, black and green, DZO sweater complete with the official Delta Zeta Theta crest on the front. I was stunned. It was beautifully done, and I would wear it with great pride in the winter months to come.

"But you hate my frat," was the only thing that I could think to say.

"But you love being a part of it," Angel answered.

And that was Angel's most defining quality: she was selfless. It didn't matter how she felt about DZO, only how I did. And if being in Delta made me happy, then she was willing to set her feelings aside and spend hours of her time to add to my enjoyment. It would take me years to truly appreciate this important quality and learn to become more selfless as well, but my feelings for her grew exponentially that night. And my opportunity to show Angel just how much came sooner than I expected.

Weather-wise, the holiday itself had been relatively mild; it wasn't even close to a white Christmas. But it wasn't long before all that changed. A week after the New Year, Long Island got walloped with a winter nor'easter that shut down both counties. Record cold, wind, and snow closed schools and many businesses for two full days. There had been advance warning, and the smart call was to stock up, hunker down, and wait for the storm to blow over; but I was 17, in love, and not all that smart.

First off, Brett and I hit the streets first thing in the morning with our snow shovels in hand, ready to dig out anybody willing to pay the freight. Shoveling snow was a great way for a young man to make money back then, and boy, did we clean up. As you know, shoveling deep, heavy snow is backbreaking work, but it's perfect for a couple of guys who were still years away from having to worry about hurting themselves. While the day was long, hard, and cold—until we worked up a sweat—the time flew with Brett by my side.

"So wait; why do they call Big John 'One Punch'?" Brett asked, begging for clarity.

"Because in his sophomore year, Jimmy O—who was a senior at the time, mind you—knocked him out cold with one punch," I repeated.

Brett thought this was hysterical.

"Well, if that's the case," Brett added, still laughing, "they should call me 'Arm Breaker'!"

Now we were both laughing.

"All right, Arm Breaker, keep shoveling."

Besides the great conversation and our endless wise-cracking, Brett had this incredible memory and would literally memorize the top comedy albums of the day; there were a bunch of them. Cheech and Chong, Firesign Theater, National Lampoon, and George Carlin all had some amazing records out at that time, and Brett knew them front to back. He could recite them so well that at times during the day, I would just have him stand on a snowbank and perform them for me—complete with his amazing voice impersonations—while I did all of the shoveling. One of my favorites was Cheech and Chong's "Dave's Not Here" routine. That one really cracked me up. I had heard all those comedy routines dozens of times before, but Brett still had me laughing until I cried.

* * *

After that long day of shoveling, I was positively desperate to see Angel —what good was a snow day if you couldn't enjoy some time with the person you most wanted to spend it with? So I asked my dad if I could borrow his car.

"Where the hell do you need to go on a night like this?" he answered in disbelief.

"I want to see Angel," I responded to what I felt was a pretty stupid question.

It was nighttime and the middle of a snowstorm...where else would I want to go?

"Nope; that's not happening," he said with a knowing chuckle.

He had been young and insane once, too.

"Why don't you walk there?" he added sarcastically; now he was actually laughing.

So I did. Such was my mania. As tired as I was, I put on all of my heaviest winter clothing—none suitable for the current nighttime arctic conditions—and headed out. Seven and a half long, brutal miles later, I arrived at Angel's door and rang the bell.

Her brother Tommy opened the inside door, saw me standing outside on the front porch looking like Sasquatch covered in snow, then closed the door on me. I couldn't believe it. From inside, I could hear him calling to his sister...

"Angel, Bobby's here!"

There were some confused muffled voices, then...

"He's at the front door!" I could hear Tommy respond from the warmth and safety inside.

He left me standing out on the front porch!

There were sounds of commotion inside, then Angel finally opened the inside door and stared out at me in disbelief. Repeating her brother's performance, she looked at me standing on the porch through the storm door.

"What are you doing here?" she asked through the glass, completely confused by my presence.

"I wanted to see you," I said, pretty confused by what was going on myself.

"Your parents lent you their car?" she asked, looking past me and clearly seeing that my parents' car was nowhere in the vicinity.

"No...," I answered, completely mystified by the welcome I wasn't getting; I was hoping for a bit more appreciation for my effort.

At this point, she should have figured it out, yet Angel continued her puzzled cross-examination.

"Then how did you get here?"

"I WALKED!" I shouted in disbelief. It was freezing.

"OH MY GOD!" she screamed. "Mom! Mom! Bobby walked here from his house!"

I guess my standing out there on her front porch under those impossible conditions was just so surreal it wasn't making sense in her head. Thankfully, it finally did, and she let me in.

"Oh my God, oh my God, oh my God," Angel fussed as she helped me out of my winter wear. "You're frozen!"

Now mom, dad, her sister Lisa Marie, and her annoying brother were all in the kitchen fawning over me and helping to warm me up. I just smiled. As tough as that long walk was, I had finally done something to show Angel how much she meant to me. I would need to redeem those brownie points I had scored that night soon enough.

CHAPTER SIXTEEN

T he problem with my split life was that while Angel brought out the best in me, my time spent with DZO definitely indulged my baser side. The angel and the devil are part of most people's personality, and if both are encouraged, they can pull hard in opposite directions.

Even though New York was one of the first states to legalize abortion in 1970, DZO decided to use the federal government's national legalization in January of 1973 as a clever theme for the annual Valentine's Day bash. We had toyed with the idea of making the end of the draft that year's theme, but as relieved as we all were not to have to go to Vietnam, it seemed hippyish and unmanly to celebrate not having to serve our country. The irony that our all-male fraternity found celebrating the legalization of a woman's right to terminate a pregnancy an acceptable theme for our dance does not escape me. By today's standards, we were all impossibly insensitive buffoons.

This yearly event wasn't just a brew-up; it was a full-on, semi-formal dance with a band and everything. Each year Delta would rent the local VFW hall and throw a legendary party. Because of the expenses incurred with an event like this, we needed to raise additional monies to make it happen. Our monthly dues and advance ticket sales alone wouldn't cover the costs. The big fundraiser was our annual "DZO Winter Cold Finger Car Wash."

Held the first Saturday in February, the entire membership would get out there and wash cars at a time of year when they really needed washing, but people just couldn't imagine actually going outside to do it for themselves. Taking your car to a car wash wasn't a big thing back then. So between driving past our homemade signs out on Grand Avenue—the main road through Baldwin—advertising the event all week, and seeing dozens of strapping young men braving the cold for an assumed "charitable cause," people lined up all day to get their cars cleaned and support our efforts. The average adult had no idea that we were raising money for a bacchanal party; our fraternity status still legitimized us in most people's eyes. Each year the annual event would financially clean up—pun fully intended—even if the car washing itself was more than a bit lacking. Most of our customers took home a car that was only slightly cleaner than when it came in, wetter, but not much cleaner.

As the Delta Valentine's Dance was considered a formal affair; everybody was expected to bring a date. Many viewed this as a romantic event. So even though Angel and I had an understanding as far as her involvement with anything frat-related went, she agreed to go with me. After more than three months, pretty much everybody knew we were going out together, and I certainly couldn't go alone or invite somebody else. I promised Angel that she would not only have a great time but would see that fraternities were not what she thought they were. The reality was they were much worse.

The night of the big event, I picked up Angel at her house, and she looked stunning. But to be fair, I didn't look too bad myself. This was 1973, and for an event like this, girls wore nice dresses—some even wore gowns—and the guys dressed in slacks, sport coats, collared shirts, and ties. The DZO Valentine's Dance was a big deal. Angel's father and mother were both there to see us off and take pictures with their Instamatic camera.

"You two have a wonderful time," Angel's mom said almost tearfully with genuine motherly affection.

"Don't make it a gun problem," her dad, Vito, whispered into my ear as I followed Angel out the front door.

At that point, it was almost his mantra; but the truth was he liked me, and his bark was way worse than his bite. The whole extended family liked me for that matter. I may not have been Italian, but I embraced their culture and love of family. My family had always been a little more...formal. We weren't very touchy-feely, and most emotions were kept in check. Heaven forbid someone says "I love you" or gives someone a hug. Having now been dating their daughter for a while and celebrating some big family holidays with the Levitanos, I had come to truly appreciate and respect the passion Italians have for life, and they had come to know and love the guy that their daughter liked so much. Unfortunately, I was about to disappoint them all big time.

Valentine's Day landed on a Wednesday that year, so the big dance was held on Saturday the 17th. It stands out to me for a bunch of reasons. When I'm waiting for an important night like that, I tend to weather watch. The days leading up to the special night were a bit rainy—which was bad—but for mid-February in New York, the weather was warmer than usual—which was good. It can be bitter cold that time of year, so temperatures in the mid-40s were considered positively balmy. By Saturday night, the rain had cleared out—which was very good—but the temperature had dropped back down into the 30s—which was so-so. All in all, it wasn't going to be too bad weather-wise for my big date with Angel.

It had been raining pretty hard that day, but the skies had completely cleared by sundown. When we arrived at the VFW hall, I walked in proudly, under a starry moonlit sky, with Angel on my arm and a shit-eating grin on my face. In many ways, it was our first official public appearance.

When we got inside, the hall was beautifully decked out with lights, streamers, balloons, and more. I was impressed. For a bunch of jocks, the decoration committee had done a pretty damn good job of setting the place up. Though I found out later that they had a lot of help from our sister sorority, which explained the feminine touches, despite the fancy front, the undertone of Delta's less-than-formal mentality was on full display with a huge, poorly-lettered banner sprawled across the wall that read:

ΔZΘ ROE V. WADE VALENTINE'S DAY DANCE
"Fuck without getting fucked!"

Angel took one look at that banner, then at me, and shook her head.

"Tell me you didn't come up with that slogan," she said.

"Of course not," I said with mock sophistication. "I wanted it to read, "Intercourse without worry.""

"Not as catchy but so much classier," Angel said.

We both laughed.

Local legends "The Dukes" were rocking the stage with their Doo-Wop show. Fifties music was the retro craze of the time, and a bunch of band and choir geeks—inspired by Woodstock wild men "Sha-Na-Na"—formed a group that packed area clubs and dances. Funny how greasy, slicked-back hair and leather jackets transformed a bunch of nerds into local stars. The band was belting out Danny and the Juniors' "At the Hop" as Angel and I entered and strolled across the room. With the exception of the offensive banner on the wall, the night was perfect.

The room was packed with rowdy DZO brothers and their dates, dancing and tearing it up along with members of other Delta-friendly Baldwin fraternities, namely the other jock frats—Beta Lambda Rho, Blue and Gold—and Tau Zeta Epsilon, the Jewish fraternity. Being a formal affair, frat jackets and colors were not allowed at the dance. As I said, the Delta Valentine's Dance was a big deal, one of the major fraternity social events of the year. I pretty much knew everybody there, and while it was definitely not Angel's social circle, she was pleasantly surprised that she knew and was friendly with a number of the other guys' dates.

Our first stop was the refreshments table to get a couple of glasses of punch. Now it shouldn't have been a surprise to anyone that the punch was spiked; it certainly wasn't to me. I well-knew my frat brothers' M.O. But Angel took one whiff of the glass I gave her and handed it right back to me.

"I think I'll pass," she said wisely. "We don't even know what they put in it."

I wasn't taken aback by the idea of drinking spiked punch, and I had a fair idea of what "they" had put in it.

"I do," I said and downed my cup in one Gavone-like gulp. "It's not that bad."

"Well, with a recommendation like that," Angel said, "definitely no."

We both laughed, then I heard a very drunk female voice slurring behind me.

"Where's Brent?" she asked.

I turned to find Aimee, Brett's dream girl, looking right through me and wavering ever so slightly.

"Oh, hey, Aimee," I said. "I think he's hanging out with some of his other friends tonight. This is my girlfriend, Angel."

It felt great to introduce someone in my world—even Aimee—to my girlfriend.

"Hi, Aimee," Angel said amicably. "I think we take Phys-Ed class together."

"Tell Brent," Aimee continued, completely ignoring Angel for no other reason than she was wasted, "tonight could have been his night."

Wow, I thought, as Aimee turned and tried to suggestively wobble away, *if Brett only knew.*

"Who's Brent?" Angel asked, completely unaffected by Aimee's less-than-warm welcome.

"Brett," I answered matter-of-factly.

"She calls Brett 'Brent'?" Angel continued her inquiry.

"Yup," I answered, already knowing her next question.

"But why doesn't he—"

"Because he wants to have sex with her," I interrupted, cutting to the chase.

It took Angel only about half of a second for this inane logic to set in.

"So if I had called you Benny, you wouldn't have corrected me?" she asked, taking her line of questioning to the bitter end.

"Probably not," I said without hesitation.

"Men," Angel said, shaking her head.

I shrugged my shoulders, not willing or able to argue her point, and we both burst out laughing again. We were having a great time.

Just then The Dukes launched into the iconic '50s classic "Earth Angel" by the Penguins; it had been my secret song for Angel since I had first laid eyes on her.

"Shall we dance?" I said formally, having fun with the moment.

"I'd be delighted," Angel replied, going with it.

With that, we strolled out onto the dance floor and faced each other, I bowed, she curtsied, then we stepped into each other's arms and began to slow dance. It really should be called "slow rocking back and forth" because that's all it actually was. Long gone were the days of young people being taught how to actually dance. All you got from any teenage couple on the dance floor back then—and even now—was a simple close embrace with minimal movement. The girl puts her arms around the boy's neck or shoulders; the guy slides his arms around her waist—or lower if he dares and she is willing—then a slow, rhythmic side-to-side motion begins like they are trying to steady themselves on rough waters; so romantic.

The lyrics of that song were seared into my soul, another one of those frozen moments in time. The song, the night, the lights, my girl; for the briefest of moments, it was picture perfect. We held each other close and felt those first sparks of what could become real love. It was like a dream.

I say "briefest of moments" because it all fell apart only minutes after it began.

"Hey, New Kid!" a voice called out loudly over the music and the crowd.

Angel and I were suddenly swarmed by Tank and a bunch of other DZO members all sans dates and feeling no pain. Our beautiful dance came to a sad halt.

"Oh, hey, Tank," I said, hoping this was only a quick interruption. "Say hi to Angel."

"We need you to settle an argument," an already inebriated Tank close-talked at me, completely ignoring my girlfriend. His breath singed my nose hairs.

"Sorry, guys, I can't do it," I said, recovering from Tank's blast. "Me and Angel are dan–"

"It will only take a second," Tank plunged on.

"No" was not going to be an acceptable answer for this bunch. He and my frat brothers literally began to herd me in the direction they wanted me to go.

"It will only take a second," he repeated as we started to move off, this time to Angel, acknowledging her presence for the first time.

"I'll be right back," I yelled over the music to my girlfriend.

"I'll be right back," Tank drunkenly assured Angel as they steered me away.

Angel looked at me shaking her head as I went, half in disbelief and half in amusement. She was now standing alone in a very crowded room.

As they dragged me off, I saw her walk over to a small group of other abandoned DZO dates, the girls that she had noticed earlier. With them, Angel found temporary solace.

The argument that needed judging was actually a contest to see who could down the most shots of alcohol in the shortest time. Being one of the more controlled drinkers in the group, along with my renowned integrity, somehow qualified me to pick a winner.

What started as Tank versus Cave Man—the president of Beta Lambda Rho—quickly devolved into an open competition as more and more members of all the frats joined in. While I wasn't one of the competitors, drinks were flowing, and I was encouraged to sample the merchandise. Drunks do not like to drink alone. Every few minutes I would try to declare a winner so I could get back to my date, but my decisions only spurred on more arguing and angrier challenges. As the judge making the bad calls, these drunken idiots physically stopped me from leaving. Yes, these were my friends, and at its core, it was a friendly competition, but the line between friends and friendly and enemies and hostility can get very blurred when alcohol is involved. But I had to get back to Angel.

Every time I tried to go, they didn't ask me to stay, they told me I was staying. And there were a lot of them. What was supposed to be Angel's and my special night out was collapsing into a typical, moronic, frat brew-up, except this time we had abandoned dates and were wearing jackets and ties.

Unbeknownst to me—I would find out the next day—at one point, Angel wandered over to see what had happened to me; she couldn't have shown up at a worse time. At that moment—I have been told—I was not only a willing participant, encouraging the next round in the competition, but I was right there in the thick of things throwing one back with the boys. Angel walked away in disgust.

Suddenly, The Dukes' stellar rendition of "Teenager In Love" was cut short when the lead singer abruptly stopped, and the band ground to a halt. This got everyone's attention. Just as suddenly, Carl's voice rang out over the PA system.

"GAMMA NU!"

Nothing more needed to be said. With that one cry, every Delta member and members of other frats attending the dance headed for the doors; and I was right there with them. This was a matter of security. Not only were Black and White attacking us, but they were doing it on a social occasion, knowing full well there would be civilians present and not expecting us to be ready for battle. Boy, were they wrong about that.

The reality was that these kinds of things occurred with regularity at brew-ups, meetings, and out on the street, but there was an unwritten rule amongst the fraternities that it wasn't allowed to happen at events like these. Still, we always had a lookout and were anything but unready. This time it was Carl. That said, the only real plan for a counterattack was to spill out of the building and fight. And that's what we did.

They say that everyone is a hero in their own story. The Crusades tortured and killed millions spreading the word of God; the Catholic Church didn't think they were evil. From their perspective, they were making the world a better place. Even a genocidal mass murderer like Adolf Hitler believed he was doing the things he did for the greater good. While I recognize the logic in those arguments, I truly believe Jimmy O was an exception to the rule. There is no doubt in my mind that he knew he was evil, wanted to be evil, and spent his days and nights thinking about, planning, and doing evil things. The man was a malicious genius and a monster.

I don't have an exact count on the Black and White members that were outside waiting for us, but there were eight cars—all double-parked in the street directly in front of the VFW hall. Figuring an average of four or five per car, that would have brought their number to around 35 or 40. Under normal circumstances, that would have been quite an army, but this was one of Baldwin Delta Zeta Theta's biggest events of the year; every member of our frat and then some was in attendance. Besides the local membership, we had DZO officers and members from Rockville Centre, Oceanside, Freeport, Uniondale, Hempstead, and even Valley Stream in attendance, with each chapter's best guys. Add to that the Delta-friendly/Gamma Nu-hating members of the other Baldwin frats that were there, and we were easily ready with triple, if not quadruple their number. So what the hell were they thinking? As it turned out, it wasn't to win.

There was literally a bottleneck of members trying to get out of the building, and as we did, we found Gamma Nu standing in wait all over the lawn, sidewalk, and street in front of the VFW hall. As all the male dance attendees exited, we lined up across the lawn and walkway, facing off with our sworn enemies. Most of us took that quiet before the storm as an opportunity to remove our sports coats (throwing them to the side or onto the ground), take off our ties, un-tuck and open our shirts, and roll up our sleeves in preparation for the fight to come. Finally, Tank walked through the front doors and stopped at the top of the stairs.

"Where the fuck are you, Jimmy O!?" Tank shouted.

As if waiting for his cue, Jimmy O dramatically stepped forward from behind a couple of Gamma Nu members and took his place at the opposite end of the walkway, facing Tank, his ever-present cigarette dangling from his lips.

"Right here, son," he said, not taking the cig out of his mouth.

"This is a social occasion on our turf," Tank continued. "Inter-fraternity law dictates events like this should be respected and are off limits to uninvited frats."

"I don't see a fraternity," Jimmy O said, scanning our ranks. "I see a bunch of dick-suckin' pussies lookin' for a beating."

This got my frat brothers and me even more fired up than we already were.

"Well then," Tank said, actually amused by Jimmy O's barb, "what are we waiting for?"

With that, he charged down the steps toward the Black and White masses.

"DELTAAAAA!" Tank roared as he ran.

The rest of us joined him in the battle cry and followed him into the battle.

"TAKE 'EM TO THE GROUND!" Jimmy O commanded his soldiers.

In the heat of this kind of fight, there is little time to look around at what others are doing. Of course, you have to keep alert for attack from all sides and try to have the back of any of your guys who are fighting nearby; but beyond that, you're simply dealing with the closest threat. This said, that night I was out for one person in particular...Jimmy O. The last couple of times our paths had crossed I'd either been alone, outnumbered, or physically unfit to fight him; this was my chance to get him on my turf with my guys to keep the fight fair. It would be just Jimmy O and me.

While the rain and clouds of the day had cleared exposing a full, moonlit sky, the ground was still soggy. As the battle ensued, combatants rolled around on the front lawn turning it and ourselves into a muddy mess; but at that moment, it was the least of our worries.

I took out the first Gamma Nu member I ran into—a simple combination of a punch in the face followed by a leg sweep brought him down—then I was blindsided by a powerful cross-body block. Crashing to the muddy ground, I looked up to see Jimmy O standing over me.

"Cunt-vacs," he said with a sneer.

Unfortunately, Big John's nickname for me was now the go-to in the wrong circles.

"Did I get your cute little outfit all dirty?" Jimmy O continued, now rubbing his hands together.

As always, he was wearing black leather gloves; but as it was now winter, they were more than just an affectation.

Never good with a snappy comeback in those situations, I gave it my best shot.

"Your outfit isn't gonna be so cute when I get done with you, O'Reilly."

As I started to get up, pondering what that even meant, Jimmy O pushed me back down with his dirt-caked boot. I slipped on the wet lawn and crashed onto the muddy ground. My cute little outfit was filthy.

"Where do you think you're going?" he taunted.

Before I could respond or even try to get up again, Jimmy O got bowled over by a hard-charging Big John who was out for blood.

"I ain't doin' this for you, New Kid!" One Shot let me know as he took Jimmy O into the dirt.

There was really no need for him to share that information with me as I had no misperception about his motivations. Like me, Big John was looking for retribution.

As I got up, I looked around to see virtually every member of Delta and Gamma Nu rolling around on the ground. It struck me as odd because most fights are from a standing position unless you're wrestling. But this time, everyone was down on the sidewalk, street, and the now torn-up, muddy lawn. Then suddenly...

"GAMMA NU! LET'S GO!" Jimmy O called the retreat to his Black and White crew.

All of Delta Gamma Nu immediately stopped fighting, got up, and ran for their cars. We ran after them but gave up the chase once their cars peeled out with all the Black and White scumbags hanging out of the windows laughing and cursing at us. One voice boomed above the rest...

"Send us the cleaning bill, pussies!" Jimmy O yelled, laughing, as he drove away.

Send us the cleaning bill? What a strange thing to say at the end of a rumble.

We were all congratulating each other on our victory; Gamma Nu had chickened out, and Delta Zeta Theta and friends had won...or so we thought. When we got back inside the hall—under the lights inside —I knew exactly what Jimmy O's parting comment meant. We were all dirty, sweaty, disgusting messes. Our nice clothes were tattered, torn, and covered in mud. Remember what I said about Jimmy O being an evil genius? He and his frat never had any intention of winning the battle; they knew they would be outnumbered. Their plan was to ruin our big dance...and they did. We were all so filthy and gross, most of our dates didn't want to go anywhere near us. And speaking of dates...where was mine?

I looked all over for Angel, hoping she would be filled with fawning admiration for my heroic efforts while The Dukes tried to get the night back on track with a crowd-pleaser, Dion and the Belmonts' "The Wanderer." But she was nowhere to be found. As I searched the hall, I became more and more frantic. Where was she?

Crossing the dance floor, I bumped into Tank who was now in a sex-and-alcohol-fueled grind to The Five Satins' hit "In the Still of the Night" with his girlfriend Joanne who didn't seem to care about how dirty and sweaty he was at all. In fact, she was reveling in it.

"Hey, Tank, have you seen Angel," I yelled to be heard over the amplifiers and PA system.

Tank was so busy applying mud and sweat to his date that he didn't even acknowledge my question. But Joanne did.

"She left," she said, with more than a hint of satisfaction.

Angel was not sorority material on any level, and it bugged the Delta sisters that I was taken by an outsider.

"She left?" I repeated in complete disbelief.

"Yup," Joanne answered. "The minute Gamma Nu arrived and the fight broke out, I saw her head for the side door. I guess your woman doesn't appreciate a real man. There are plenty of Theta girls who do."

That drove the knife deep into my heart. Angel left the dance without me. Then again, why wouldn't she? As far as she knew, I had abandoned her to party with my friends and then got into a brawl. It was everything she hated.

I should have left the dance immediately and gone after her, but I didn't. I'm not sure why: embarrassment, shame, anger, frustration; maybe all of the above. While I was wrestling with the emotions running through my head, Delta was still celebrating our so-called victory over Gamma Nu, taking the party to the next level. With alcohol, testosterone, and adrenaline coursing through everyone's veins, it wasn't long before the "ΔZΘ Roe v. Wade Valentine's Dance" had degraded into a drunken, rowdy near-riot. And I'm embarrassed to say...I was right there with them.

When The Dukes finally played their last song of the night, "Rock 'n' Roll Is Here to Stay" by Danny and the Juniors, some of us weren't ready for the evening to end. We definitely didn't feel like we got any satisfaction earlier in the night, and by then, everyone had realized Black and White's true motivation for crashing our dance. My frat brothers and I were pumped up, feeling no pain, and looking for some payback. All of the wrong stars were aligned.

Tank drunkenly climbed onto the stage and grabbed the mic.

"Delta! Let's go beat some Gamma Nu ass!"

This got a drunken roar from the membership still in the room. The more sober ones had already wisely left with their dates, heading out to hopefully plow much greener pastures. But the remaining members of

DZO charged outside, piled into cars, and began cruising the town. We were out for Black and White blood.

There is no rage like a male, drunken, testosterone-fueled rage. Add adrenalin, youth, and stupidity to that mix, and you've got a potentially lethal combination. Considering how often that nightmarish mixture comes together, it's amazing many men survive their early years to proliferate the species.

What started out as five angry Delta carloads slowly whittled itself down to one: mine. As we drove up and down, street after street after street, some got bored and/or sobered up and lost their motivation, while still others remembered they had dates. If there was any chance left of getting some action from their girls, they knew that they needed to get back to the dance and pick them up pronto. But not the car I was in. This car had the jewels of the stupidity crown in it: Tank, Big John, Cave Man, the Joey Crack—were all in this car—and me. Of the five of us, I would realize later, I was the stupidest. I know the proper phrasing of that statement is "I was the most stupid," but when you are that stupid using proper grammar seems like you're putting on airs. That may be funny, but you will soon see that it wasn't funny at all.

While the others were just mean teenage bullies—who would eventually grow up to be mean adult bullies and raise mean teenage bully sons—I was in foreign territory. This wasn't my way by nature; it wasn't who I really was. My anger was driven by love, frustration, and confusion...and fueled by liquor. These were alien feelings to me that I hadn't experienced before, didn't understand, and had no idea how to manage. So, with the help of demon alcohol, they expressed themselves in hostility and rage. And it was catastrophic.

As we continued to cruise the main drags and neighborhoods, we kept drinking. If you're going to nurse an alcohol-fueled rage, you gotta keep on fueling it with alcohol. The longer we drove, the more desperate we became to "fuck up some Gamma Nu." It got to the point that we were jumping out of the car and chasing just about any male of the right age walking the streets. Some we pushed and shoved, but when we would realize they had nothing to do with Black and White, we'd get back into our car and drive off to continue the search. The more we drove, the drunker, angrier, and stupider we got.

Places like "The Woods" near my house were not exclusive to my neighborhood. A lot of areas in a lot of towns have wooded areas. These are not planned forested lots created and maintained by the community or the local parks department. They are simply undeveloped properties that have yet to be exploited by the property owners. Case in point, The Woods in my neighborhood has since been knocked down and built on; it is no longer the habitat of young imaginations and troublemakers. Sad really.

Eventually, our anger cruise brought us past the darkened woods of a neighborhood where through the leafless winter trees...we saw a campfire.

"GAMMA NU!" Tank screamed.

"GAMMA NU!" the rest of us joined him in yelling.

Crack drove his car up and over the nearest curb, and the five of us jumped out and ran into the woods heading in the direction of the flames. Finally, we would have some revenge. Keeping our voices to an intoxicated whisper, we quickly advanced toward our targets. From the vantage point of the trees and bushes we were hiding behind, we could see there were only four of them, gathered around a small fire, laughing like idiots. We had them outnumbered. Tank silently communicated for us to surround them and wait for his signal.

Even though it was dark, and the fire only lit the Gamma Nu members in silhouette, my sober subconscious brain told me something was wrong. The actions of our unsuspecting victims were anything but cool frat guys—they were way too silly—and for the life of me I could not see any sign of their Black and White colors. No self-respecting member of any fraternity would hang out with his 'brothers' and not wear his colors. Then again, most of the Gamma Nu members who came to the sit-down weren't wearing colors. But there was something oddly familiar about this bunch. It was very dark, and even though that little voice in my head was frantically waving a red flag, I was still too drunk, mad, and ready for a fight for any of it to really register. Then...

"GET 'EM!" Tank's angry roar cut through the cold night air.

The five of us charged our unsuspecting victims from all sides and started punching and kicking. As I came up behind my target, I couldn't believe he was just standing, arms hanging at his sides, watching his brothers being beaten up. *He must be in shock*, I said to myself. But still...

Something else registered with my subconscious but failed to have any effect on my mission as my soon-to-be opponent wasn't very large. Black and White liked to recruit them big, but as I pounced, all of these clues had still not formed into the logical conclusion in my mind that these guys were not members of Delta Gamma Nu. I spun the opponent around, turning him into the dark as I brought my fist down on his barely visible, but clearly terrified, face.

"Bobby?!" an anguished, disbelieving voice said milliseconds before my fist connected with his nose, instantly breaking it. It was Brett.

He fell to the ground holding his face, rocking in pain, blood flowing everywhere. Instantly sober, I looked around at the other "Gamma Nu members"—all beaten and lying on the ground. It was Ronnie, Tommy, and Timmy. We had jumped The Bretts. Made men.

As the true horror of what I had done was setting in...

"LET'S GO!" Tank barked, and he and the other three turned and ran from the carnage, laughing and cheering as they went.

I hesitated, trying to figure out what the hell I should do. By now, all of The Bretts were staring at me in shock and disbelief.

"I'm sorry," I said in a hoarse whisper.

It was all I could think to say or do.

Then like a coward—mortified by my actions and inaction—I ran after the others, leaving my real friends alone to deal with their pain and humiliation. Yes, humiliation. The pain goes away, and the wounds eventually heal, but the humiliation and embarrassment of having been beaten up—unable or unwilling to fight back—is something that emotionally scars you for a lifetime.

And Brett's shame would change him forever.

CHAPTER SEVENTEEN

By the time we got back to the VFW hall, I was completely sober, and the full magnitude of my actions had hit me. Besides the Brett situation—if besides was even an acceptable word for an unspeakable action like that—the reality of how badly I had screwed up with Angel was starting to set in. Climbing into my parents' car, I decided to deal with that situation first and address the Brett disaster later. Surely, he was in some emergency room getting his nose fixed.

It was now after midnight, so there was no way I could simply knock on the front door of Angel's house and just talk to her. Besides, I wasn't sure what her father knew or didn't know. The idea of him greeting me with a bat, or worse, wasn't very appealing. Throwing rocks at her window was an option, but the odds were she was furious with me. Waking her up to have some strained whispered fight with me standing in the side yard and her hanging out of a second-story window into the now-freezing night didn't feel like the best course of action, either.

I stopped off at the local Dunkin Donuts, grabbed four jumbo cups of coffee and a mixed dozen of borderline stale donuts—the freshly-baked ones wouldn't come out for another couple of hours—and headed to Angel's house. Once there, I parked out front, drank coffee, ate donuts, and waited. She would eventually have to leave the house, and I would be there to intercept her.

Sitting and waiting as I did for the next several hours gave me a chance to reflect on how incredibly stupid I had been the night before and truly suffered for my sins. In just a few short hours, I had managed to offend—and maybe lose—the girl of my dreams and beat up and injure the best friend I ever had. Sure, I had excuses for my behavior; but when I went over them in my head, they all seemed really pathetic, because they were.

At around nine o'clock in the morning, Angel's visiting grandmother —her mother's mother—finally opened the front door to sweep something out onto the stoop. It's an odd cleaning method. When you sweep something out the door, it doesn't go away, it simply sits there waiting for someone to step in it and track it back into the house. Grandma saw me sitting in the car, shook her head in disbelief, and went back inside. Moments later, a sleepy-eyed Angel wearing a bathrobe peered out of the door. Echoing her grandmother's feelings, she too shook her head and went back in. Nursing my fourth, now lukewarm cup of coffee and eating just the edges of my last donut— powdered lemon custard filled, my least favorite—I desperately wanted to apologize and beg for her forgiveness. I also badly needed to use a bathroom. Thankfully, I didn't have to wait too long.

A short time later the front door of the Levitano house opened and out came a jean, t-shirt, and sneaker-clad Angel covered in her dad's giant parka thrown on to keep warm. Having just woken up, with no makeup and her hair a mess, she still looked stunning. Angel opened the passenger door of my car and got in. Up close, she was even more beautiful...and I could feel the disgust radiating off of her.

"Start talking," she said, barely controlling her rage.

And I did.

I can't remember exactly what I said early that Sunday morning, but do I really need to? It had to be the same things said, since the beginning of time, to billions of girls by billions of guys who have messed up and want "just one more chance." I'm sure even the cavemen had been in that situation. I swore to her nothing like that would ever happen again. Sadly, moronic guys like me don't learn easily.

Before she let me off the hook, Angel asked one final question...

"So what's the deal with you and that guy from the Oceanside fraternity? Why are you so obsessed with him?"

The answer was simple: self-preservation. Jimmy O had been after me since the day I stood up for Brett and sullied his shitty reputation. Since then he and his crew had been trying to get even with me, promising each time they failed that my day would come. The guy's actions forced me to join a fraternity I didn't want to be a part of and had me constantly looking over my shoulder; he wouldn't stop until he made good on his threat. The only way to put an end to the continuing harassment was for me to confront Jimmy O once and for all.

"But violence leads to more violence," Angel said, stating the obvious. "This all started with Jimmy O's attack on Brett, then your attack on him, then him trying to get even with you. Do you really think the answer is more violence?"

"No, I don't," I replied, "but what other choices do I have, leave town?"

"Not until after we graduate," she said with a coy smile.

Angel had forgiven me.

* * *

Why I thought that I could take the same path—sans donuts and coffee—with Brett was beyond me. I hadn't just broken his nose...I broke his heart. The fact that later that same day I had the audacity to actually go to his house and knock on the front door speaks volumes about my true lack of understanding of just how bad my actions were.

Sure, I got the basics—betrayal and assault—but the depth of my violation had really not gotten through my thick head. It started to when his mother and father answered the door. I could feel the heat of their hatred before they even said a word.

"Hi, Mr. and Mrs. Pearson, is–" I started.

"What the hell do you want?" Mr. Pearson said, cutting me off.

"I just wanted to see how Brett is doing and ta–"

"How dare you touch my son!" Mrs. Pearson jumped in, her motherly protective hostility pouring off of her.

"Touch?" Mr. Pearson joined in on the verbal beating. "That was assault. You assaulted our son and shattered his nose. He had to have surgery to reconstruct it."

Surgery? I started to apologize.

"I'm so sorry about what hap–"

"Don't you dare go anywhere near my Brett ever again!" Mrs. Pearson said, barely controlling her rage.

"Fuck that," Mr. Pearson added, taking the kid gloves completely off. "I filed assault charges against you with the police this morning, and we are getting a court order of protection to keep you away from him. You should be hearing from the authorities very soon."

And they did. The police arrived at my house a short time later, taking the retribution for my night of drunken stupidity to a whole new level. Now my parents were completely brought up to speed on everything I had done. To say they weren't happy is an insult to each of those words.

Unfortunately, the assault itself was viewed as harassment and written off as high school tomfoolery. I say unfortunately because, while it was in fact very fortunate for me, once again it spoke volumes about the lack of seriousness the local authorities had toward the bullying actions and stupidity of the fraternities. Many of the things being done by the frats had potentially lethal consequences, yet they were consistently dismissed as hijinks. This was an ongoing mistake.

While I was spared being arrested and having to deal with a court trial and a possible criminal record, the order of protection against me was issued, and my parents came down on me hard, but not as hard as they should have. Sure, I was grounded and banned from using their car, but like the police, my dad still compared my missteps to his own wanton youth; and considering the severity of what I had done, for the most part, he let me slide. I really wish he hadn't.

So, did I quit Delta? I wanted to. I needed to. They were a detriment to all of my relationships, health, and well-being. But I couldn't for the same reason I was forced to join them in the first place: Jimmy O.

* * *

Shortly after that fateful night to remember, I came home one afternoon after school and, as usual, was greeted by my mom when I walked into the kitchen. This time she had news to tell me.

"Your friend stopped by today," she said.

"My friend?" I asked intrigued.

Other than Brett—who I couldn't have paid to stop by—I had nobody else in that "stop by the house" category.

"Yes. He was a really nice young man," my mother continued. "We had tea."

Now I was completely confused.

"You had tea with a friend of mine who stopped over?" I pushed. "Tea?"

"Why are you so surprised?" she asked. "I am capable of having a conversation with one of your friends, Bobby."

"But who was it, Mom?"

"James," she responded.

I quickly ran through the Rolodex of friends and associates in my head. For the life of me, I could not think of a James who would fit that bill. And what was this James doing out of school?

"James who?" I asked.

"James O'Reilly," she replied matter-of-factly.

Jimmy O? Jimmy O!? Jimmy O had come to my house, knocked on my door, and had tea with my mother! I tried to be casual; I didn't want to worry her or let her know what a potential danger this guy was. A few years later, the true darkness of what Jimmy O was capable of would be revealed; and thinking back on it now, I am even more horrified by the thought of what could have happened to my mother that day. As I said, Jimmy O was truly evil.

"Did he say anything, leave a message for me?" I asked, keeping as calm as I could.

"No. He just stopped by to say hello," my mother replied, already back working at whatever it was she was doing in the kitchen before I arrived. "Oh wait, yes. He said to tell you that he was looking for you."

He was looking for me. And that's why I didn't—why I couldn't—quit Black and Green. Because that psychopath Jimmy O had come to my house—*my house!*—and left a message with my mother that he was looking for me! That piece of shit was fucking with me, and his message was loud and clear: I know where you live.

I still needed protection. I still needed my fraternal brothers. Thankfully, my frat life had stabilized for the most part. Sure, there were regular brew-ups and meetings, but I had sworn off drinking since that eventful Valentine's Day night, so while things weren't nearly as exciting, they never got completely out of hand either. And things stayed relatively calm. But being in a fraternity was like that, it ebbed and flowed. After every catastrophic or near-catastrophic event, things would quiet down for a bit. So, Delta was in an ebbing period for a time...but it wasn't long before things started to flow again.

* * *

Besides my relationship being on track with Angel—and when I say "besides" I mean Angel was my number one focus with a bullet—the other bright spot in my life was playing lacrosse. I had tried out for and made the team just before the DZO Valentine's Dance events. I guess I really was "Baldwin Varsity material" as Coach Landers had said. Practices were already underway, and due to the character-building qualities of intramural sports, continuing to play was thankfully not included in my parents' grounding.

Running around a field "checking" people with your lacrosse stick and knocking people on their asses was a great way to let off steam. Anger and frustration had become a big part of my day-to-day life since that terrible night; I really needed a way to let it out. And it kept me out of trouble, too.

* * *

Dates and spending time with Angel became a lot easier when I was allowed to use the money I had saved to get a car of my own: a 1965 Honey Gold Ford Galaxy with an automatic transmission, a 289 V-8, and a front "bench seat" perfect for sitting right up close to your girl. Sure, it was what we called a beater with a lot of rust, and it required both water and oil at virtually every stop I made for gas, but this was before the Arab Oil Embargo of '74. A kid could afford to have a car like that. You could still find gas for less than 30 cents a gallon and buy a quart of oil for twenty-five cents. That's a full case of the stuff for just six bucks. The car wasn't much to look at either, but she was all mine, and I had big plans for ol' "Seabiscuit" come the summer. Custom rims, white letter racing tires...I was going to really do her up. Unfortunately, I never got the chance.

With transportation now always at the ready, Angel and I got to do so much more together. Whether it was big things or little things, I no longer had to ask to borrow my parents' car—which I had been banned from using anyway—or get a ride from someone; I'd just jump in my ride and pick up my girl whenever I needed. That's when you first realize that having a real relationship with someone isn't just about the big dates and special events; it's the other, smaller, in-between moments you spend together that create your bond. And after five months of going out with Angel, we had developed a real relationship.

Angel wasn't much of a sports fan—especially of lacrosse—but to her credit, she came to every one of my games; and at some of those early March matches, it got pretty cold. She knew nothing about lacrosse, and there was many a time that I'd catch her cheering for the other team, thinking that something good had just happened for the Baldwin Bruins. But just seeing her in the stands, rooting me on, was a much-needed physical manifestation of having someone in my corner. Sure, I was still a part of Delta and my brothers—some of who were on my lacrosse team—would always have my back, but those relationships had no real depth or feelings. We were there for each other because that's what was expected. For example, Big John hated my guts —he disliked me from the moment we met—but "his blood ran Black and Green" and he would have come to my defense at any time if he got the call. The relationship between Angel and me existed not because it had to but because we wanted it to. I wanted to be with her, and she wanted to be with me. This was an incredible feeling that I never wanted to lose.

Angel and lacrosse aside, there was still one thing that had completely changed for the worse and remained that way, my relationship with Brett. Not only was it over, but he had virtually disappeared from the world that I knew. I didn't need to keep away from him because I hardly ever saw him anywhere. Not in the neighborhood, coming or going to school, or anywhere on the school grounds or around town. When I did, it was just brief glimpses as he rode away or turned a corner. He even stopped eating lunch with the other Bretts, who were avoiding me like the plague as well, but they still sat at their table during fifth-period lunch. Not Brett. I don't know if he changed his schedule, was eating outside of school, or what, but there was no doubt he was keeping far away from me.

* * *

It was the last week of March and while temperature-wise the month was "going out like a lamb," unfortunately the "April Showers" were already kicking in. With the rain pouring down and Angel by my side, I had just pulled "Seabiscuit" into a spot in the school's student parking lot when three of my Delta brothers went running by. I could tell by their urgency that they weren't just rushing to get out of the rain. Joey "Drummer" was bringing up the rear.

"Hey, Stefko, what's going on?" I shouted, rolling down the window as he passed. My face was immediately wet.

"It's Gamma Nu!" he answered as he continued to run.

I didn't need to hear anything else.

"Sorry, Angel, I've got to go," I barked as I jumped out of the car.

"Bobby, wait...," she started to implore.

"I'll catch you fourth period," I shouted back as I took off.

I don't know if she said anything after that, I just ran after Drummer and the others getting soaked as I went. I knew that the situation was as serious as it got. Black and White were on our school grounds during school hours; that couldn't be a good thing.

When I arrived at the front of the school, there was already a small army of DZO guys there standing in the downpour along with members of Beta Lambda Rho, Sigma Lambda Rho, and Black and Grey. This was as much an affront to them as it was to us. Directly across the street from the entrance—not actually on school grounds, so technically they weren't trespassing—was a sea of Black and White with Jimmy O front and center. Even dripping wet, somehow the cigarette dangling out of his smug mouth stayed lit. This was more Gamma Nu than I had ever seen in one place before.

The Baldwin frats lined up across the front of the school in a defensive position, prepared for action. Between all of us, we had to have been over 100 strong, everyone ready to face off with our adversaries. Anticipating a battle royal, any students and teachers who remained outside scattered. In the distance, we could already hear police sirens making their opinion known.

Suddenly, Jimmy O started a slow clap; the slap of his wet, black leather-gloved hands amplified the action, making it even more powerful. The other Gamma Nu members quickly joined him. As the volume and speed of the slow clap built, the legion of Black and White parted, and a small group of about 15 emerged from the pack and headed straight for us.

Everyone on the Baldwin side was confused by this focused action, not really sure of what was going on; but we stood fast.

"Hey, Cunt-vacs," Jimmy O shouted, singling me out. "Do you miss him?"

Miss him? Miss who, I thought.

As usual, Jimmy O's timing was perfect because just then the Gamma Nu member at the front of the approaching pack came into view. It was Brett. *My Brett!*

Drenched and wearing a brand-new Black and White jacket, he blank-stared right at me as he approached. This was the first time I had really seen him since the incident in the woods, and he looked completely out of place as a member of Gamma Nu, like some little kid playing grownup. Thankfully, his nose looked good.

As other members of our frats began to pick out various Baldwin High alumni in the pack, awareness of what was happening came to most of us pretty much simultaneously. This was the Baldwin chapter of Delta Gamma Nu. The mass of Black and White members standing across the street was their escort to make sure nobody messed with their brothers.

"That's right, dorks, let 'em pass," Jimmy O goaded. "Any of you losers touch any of the members of our newest chapter, and there will be a war."

"I'm sure we can handle whatever you got!" Tank shouted, piercing the hammering rain as he stepped to the front of our allied forces.

"Are you sure you're sure, William?" Jimmy O responded with a smirk, suggesting he knew something we didn't.

There had been rumors going around that Gamma Nu had been hard at work beefing up their rank and file. The presence of a Baldwin chapter backed up this notion. And unlike the other frats, Black and White's graduating members—and I use that term very loosely—tended to continue to be very active in the club even after they left school. A lot of them dropped out, and only a few went on to college or even left home. Since most of them were still local, they were more than happy to hang out and fight with their old frat brothers if called upon.

"Brett," I called to my friend urgently when he got closer.

No response. He and the other Baldwin Gamma Nu members soldiered through without even acknowledging we were there.

"C'mon, Brett, this isn't you," I said again as he passed, reaching out and grabbing his shoulder.

He violently threw my hand off.

"Keep your fucking hands off me, Cunt-vacs," Brett hissed, and like the rain, his hatred for me poured out of him.

This was my fault. I had driven him to take this desperate action. As I had joined Delta to protect myself from Gamma Nu, now Brett had joined Black and White to protect himself from *me*. Brett had gone from being my best friend to one of the new enemies within. I couldn't believe what I was seeing. I just stood there in the rain, dripping wet, as the best friend I ever had turned away and walked inside.

Remember what I said about Jimmy O being truly evil? Well, I found out later that when he heard about what I had done to Brett, he took full advantage of the situation and went out of his way to befriend him. How much must Brett have hated me to join up with the guy who had broken his arm? Jimmy O took Brett under his wing, grooming him to be "true Gamma Nu," whatever the hell that was. The word was that Brett didn't have to do a day of dogging or even go through a Hell Night. He just put on a Black and White jacket, and he was in. The great manipulator Jimmy O was using Brett to get even with me. And it was working.

Later that day I saw Brett walking down the hall with a cigarette behind his ear and the neck of a beer bottle sticking out of the pocket of his jacket. As we passed each other, I couldn't help myself. I reached out and grabbed his arm as he walked by.

"Brett," I said urgently.

"I thought I told you to keep your fucking hands off of me, Cunt-vacs?!" he yelled as he spun away and took a couple of steps back.

"C'mon, man," I implored as I moved toward him.

"What are you gonna do, hit me again...friend?" Brett asked. "GAMMA NU!"

Within seconds other Black and White members and allies—mainly Beta Kappa Phi and Black and Purple—rushed to his aid and surrounded us. Members of DZO reacted just as quickly and surrounded them. It was a standoff.

"I just want to talk to you," I practically begged.

"Don't be such a fucking pussy," Brett said. "We've got nothing to talk about."

With that, he turned and walked off with his new crew.

* * *

The memory of my actions and the sad change in my former friend haunted me. Sure, I still had Angel and she definitely made me feel better. But she couldn't alter or even argue the fact that what I had done was pretty much the shittiest thing imaginable, and I just couldn't stop blaming myself for what had happened and what was happening to Brett now. Who else was there to blame...besides Jimmy O?

We all make mistakes. Some are little, some are big, and some are monstrous. Depending on their significance, they can haunt us, hanging around in our conscious or subconscious for hours, days, weeks, or more. Much more. Usually, we are afforded the luxury of not thinking about it or at least not thinking about it from time to time. The further we get from the actual screw-up, the less its memory preys on us. The spaces between our remembering grow greater and greater until it becomes one of those things we look back on with regret, but the lasting effects of our actions have thankfully faded away to almost nothing. But for some misdeeds, that's not even close to the truth.

The memory of what I did to Brett not only didn't fade, it lived next door to me, went to school with me, and was there as a constant reminder of just how awful I had been to someone I cared about and who had cared so much about me. I could not forget it or forgive myself for even a second. And within a few short days, the nightmare I had started grew to an unfathomable level.

CHAPTER EIGHTEEN

FOOL'S DAY KILLERS CAPTURED

By Mark Segal - Updated April 5, 1973 - 7:36 PM

Two Nassau County high school students are being held without bail today after their arrest for allegedly killing a homeless veteran Sunday afternoon following a drunken vandalism spree that turned violent, Oceanside police said.

The Nassau County District Attorney's Office and police identified the suspects, both of whom are 17 years old, as Brett "The Weasel" Pearson of Baldwin and Dave "Stash" Sullivan of Oceanside. Police said the suspects were both arrested yesterday and charged with second-degree murder and third-degree criminal mischief.

Pearson and Sullivan were remanded to the Nassau County Jail without bail during their appearance in First District Court in Mineola, according to court records.

Messages seeking comment left with the parents of both suspects were not immediately returned.

Police said that on April 1, the teens vandalized several school buses and property belonging to the Baumann Bus Company on Lawson Blvd. in Oceanside.

Pearson and Sullivan, who are members of Delta Gamma Nu high school fraternity, encountered Dale Taveras, a 41-year-old Korean War vet, who they found unconscious along the side of the bus company warehouse. After first urinating on the man, they used a large piece of broken concrete to crush the sleeping vet's skull, causing his death, police said.

Pearson and Sullivan were located and arrested by the authorities near their respective schools Thursday morning at approximately 10:30 a.m.

Continued on page A7

And that's how I heard. Through the news media like everybody else. I just couldn't, I wouldn't, believe it. I knew there was no way—no matter how far Brett had fallen—he could ever be capable of killing someone. But somehow he was connected to this awful crime, and I knew—even though Brett wanted nothing to do with me—that if I had been there with him, it never would have happened. I would have given my life to stop him from taking the actions that led him to be a part of such a tragedy. It's what he would have done for me.

Even though Brett and Stash had not been convicted, the press had already nicknamed them the "The April Fools Killers," cementing the public's opinion before they were even tried. The only other information available about what had happened was from the ever-churning rumor mill, which generated far more fiction than fact. The one bit that came through loud and clear was that Brett and Stash had not been alone; multiple people had seen Jimmy O with them the day it happened. I knew that somehow that lowlife had to be responsible. This was a whole new level of evil for even him, but if somebody was going to commit a murder on April Fool's Day, it would have been right up his sick, demented alley.

Due to the severity and brutality of the crime, Brett and Stash remained in custody the entire time leading up to their trial. This was a nightmare. Brett had a lot of heart, but he wasn't a big or tough guy; I feared for his wellbeing on every level and had nightmares imagining what he might be dealing with in the Nassau County Jail while he awaited trial. Nassau was a local prison, but that didn't mean it wasn't filled with some really bad people and a very dangerous place for someone like Brett to be.

* * *

It was over a year before Brett's case went to trial, long after the story I'm telling you was finished, but I'm not going to make you wait to hear the fate of my poor friend.

During all the time Brett was in prison, I was unable to communicate with him for a variety of reasons—and believe me, I tried. I went to visit him in jail on numerous occasions, but I was turned away every time. Brett needed all the help and friends he could get, yet he still wanted absolutely nothing to do with me...and I couldn't blame him.

Because the crime was so heinous, Brett and Stash were tried separately as adults, even though neither of them was 18 at the time they allegedly committed the crimes. If convicted, Brett was looking at a possible life sentence. I knew any extended jail time would be a veritable death sentence for my former friend.

When the trial finally happened, the newspapers, radio, and television news were filled with April Fool's Killers headlines and sound bites, most presuming Brett and Stash's guilt, not their innocence. As I couldn't attend the trial—for reasons completely out of my control—I only found out the full story long after the verdict was delivered.

After more than a week of Brett being crucified by the attorneys for the state—and made out to be "everything wrong with young people today"—Brett's lawyers finally got their chance to offer his defense. They presented a very different version of Brett and a whole other story.

According to Brett and Stash, they had in fact been hanging out with Jimmy O that afternoon drinking and getting high. The three had spent the day walking down and around the desolate Lawson Boulevard looking for trouble. Being a Sunday, the road and workplaces in that factory area were fairly desolate. At some point—time being very abstract when you're high—the three jumped the rear fence into the Baumann Bus Company yard and began committing acts of vandalism on the bright yellow vehicles parked there, basic cretinous teenage behavior. Baumann did have a yard security guard on duty that day, but he was easily avoided in the acres of buses. After their rampage, they broke into the Baumann building and continued their spree in the garage, machine shop, and offices inside. When they were done, they hopped over the fence on the north side of the yard to leave and encountered a homeless man lying on the ground, passed out drunk, "sleeping it off" along the wall of the Baumann building. He was still holding a near-empty bottle of Thunderbird he'd obviously been drinking.

Remember what I said about Jimmy O being truly evil? Well, this is when things got really dark.

Suddenly, Jimmy O snarled, "Let's kill him."

Brett and Stash laughed at the comment, not thinking for a second he was serious. They wouldn't believe even Jimmy O could be that bad. That's when Stash came up with an idea.

"Let's piss on him," Stash said. "When he wakes up, he'll think he pissed himself...a lot."

Laughing their heads off as they did, Brett and Stash each took out their "manhood" and proceeded to urinate all over the poor unconscious drunk, when suddenly...

"Incoming!" Jimmy O's voice cut through the air from above.

Brett and Stash looked up to see Jimmy O laughing on the roof of the Baumann building, holding a large chunk of concrete over the edge with his gloved hands. Before either of them could call out for him to stop, he let the piece of cement go, and it came crashing down— narrowly missing Brett and Stash—onto the homeless man's head, caving in his skull.

Praying that it wasn't as bad as it looked and already too late, Brett and Stash desperately lifted the cement piece off the man's smashed head trying to help the poor guy—who was beyond help—and in the process left more trace evidence all over the crime scene. Jimmy O watched the aftermath of his deadly action for a quick minute, laughing in amusement at the boys' desperation.

"April Fools!" he shouted down at his friends, then he walked off, leaving them to take the fall.

Unable to help the innocent victim, Brett and Stash panicked and took off, too. They were arrested three days later for a crime they had not committed.

Detectives investigated the boys' assertion of Jimmy O's involvement but found no prints or any other evidence on or around the murder scene. Remember Jimmy O's gloves? Jimmy O admitted to hanging out with Brett and Dave earlier in the day but claimed to have left for home long before the murder was committed to do his schoolwork. *Schoolwork!?* With Jimmy O's school record and rap sheet admitted as evidence, no one believed it for a second, but he had a rock-solid alibi. His mother swore that her sweet boy was home doing that exact thing at the time of the murder.

You've got to feel for the moms of criminals. They give birth to beautiful babies and dream of the greatness their child might achieve, only to one day wind up sitting in some courtroom crying about how their "baby" is "a good boy" or "a good girl."

In the end. it was Brett and Stash's words against Jimmy O and his mother.

The saddest and truest moment of all was when Brett—now "jail sober" and back to his old self—took the stand as a last-ditch effort to vindicate himself and preserve his freedom. Angel, who had attended the trial, said that he was so pitifully sad during his testimony—actually breaking down and sobbing—you couldn't help but believe him. But with all the physical evidence still pointing directly at Brett, the jury had no choice but to convict him, though on the lesser charge of manslaughter. The judge, following the jury's leniency, sentenced Brett to time served and five years' probation. While he at least was released from prison immediately after the verdict, Brett still had a criminal record for murder and the scars of his incarceration. He would carry both the rest of his life and forever be a shadow of his former self.

If not for meeting me, none of that would have ever happened.

But before Brett's sentencing day, I had major problems of my own, problems that prevented me from attending Brett's trial and nearly destroyed my life. And like Brett, I owed it all to Jimmy O.

CHAPTER NINETEEN

With Brett sitting in prison waiting to be tried for murder, the guilt I carried for him and his situation was insurmountable. Replaying the events leading to his arrest over and over in my head, there was no denying I was at the head of the trail that led Brett to his ruin. From the day we met to when I jumped him in the woods, if you connected all the dots and the subsequent Gamma Nu events, there was no denying my culpability. I was a shitty friend and had ruined Brett's life. Sure, Jimmy O held a lot of the blame; this whole mess started when he broke Brett's arm and I came to the rescue. But Jimmy O wasn't Brett's best friend, and since then, I made so many wrong choices that I just couldn't let myself off the hook. The thoughts of what he was dealing with every day and night in prison created terrifying images in my mind. We've all seen movies and TV shows, read articles, and heard stories. We know what happens to small, young men in prisons. And there was nothing I could do to help him.

While I could find distractions during the day, every night as I lay in bed, Brett's tragedy played on a loop in my mind, literally driving me insane. The idea of him alone, afraid, and violated in some cell...I just couldn't get the horrible thoughts out of my head. Night after night, I lay awake thinking about it as the building sleep deprivation hastened my decline. How can you think straight when you can barely think at all? In the end, the only way I could ease my mental suffering was to self-medicate. Judge me if you want, but I never claimed to be the strongest man in the world, and I certainly wasn't the first or last to turn to alcohol or drugs to try and forget. And that's when pretty much everything in my life went completely south.

* * *

My first line of defense in my upbringing had always been my mom and dad; they taught me right from wrong and kicked me back into play whenever I drifted from their guidelines. Being an Air Force man, my dad was always in command, strict even by military father standards. My mother usually acted as a counterbalance to my dad's rigidness, being more loving and nurturing, but she could always step up her own toughness if she felt my dad was going too easy on me and it was needed. And speaking of counterbalances, I can't forget my kid sister.

I realize now that Suzy was always there running interference for me with my parents. She may have been six years younger, but somehow she always seemed to know when I needed to be saved and would either do something incredibly "toddler cute" or, when she got older, interject with some seemingly urgent need at just the right moment. I'll always love her for that.

This family quadrangle tried and succeeded, for the most part, in providing me with the stability and balance that I needed to grow up straight and strong. Until I hit 18 years old and legally became an adult.

From my father's strict military point of view, if I was old enough to drink, drive, vote, and fight for my country, I was a man and could and should handle my own affairs. Hell, he had already informed me that as of that coming summer I was expected to pay rent for living in their house. Like I said...strict. While he was incredibly disappointed and angry with me for my actions and behaviors that last semester, my father firmly believed it was no longer his place to interfere.

My mother, on the other hand, being the far more logical of the two, fully realized that just because I had reached some arbitrary number did not mean I was necessarily capable of handling everything life might throw my way. But my father's "old enough to..." argument was a tough one to beat, and she was hard-pressed to enforce any real punishments or effect any significant changes in me. Remember what I said about the mothers of criminals in court? Sadly, all my mom could do was stand by and suffer as she watched me desperately trying to swim in treacherous waters...and I was drowning. Her hurt and obvious disappointment just added to the failure I already felt, but it still was not enough to change what was becoming a self-destructive course of action.

At the time I wasn't sure—and didn't care—why my parents were being so lenient. To be free to live your own life was a childhood dream come true. But to paraphrase the lyrics of Alice Cooper's "I'm 18," I was a boy, and I was a man. Looking back on it now, I can see that their lack of authority during my emotional decline was part of a perfect storm of events leading to my ruin. I'm not blaming it on them, but it was a lot to handle myself...and I couldn't. I was floundering and needed help, but I didn't ask for it. And I wouldn't until it was way too late.

Now, most adults don't realize the powerful influence school and the outside world has on their kids. They get it on a superficial, obvious level, but there's a whole other education and many life-changing experiences that happen during those seven hours or so that they are actually in school and going to and from. For some kids, that comes to about 10 hours a day completely out of their parents' sphere of influence. Add to that after-school activities and eight-ish hours of sleep each night and you are realistically looking at maybe four hours of controlled parenting time. And of that four hours, how much of it is actually one on one, mother/father/child interaction? Those few hours dwindle over the years and by high school, the parents' influence comes down to maybe a shouted, "Make good choices!" as their teen bolts out the front door. And what exactly are your kids learning while out in the real world and "walking the halls of knowledge?"

Leaving the house each morning, I was reinserted into the very world and environment that had corrupted and brought me to ruin in the first place. While my parents could exert little or no influence over me, at least at home I was momentarily safe—if you overlook the occasional afternoon tea with Jimmy O—from what was becoming a more and more hostile and dangerous environment. Outside was where the gang-like frat world was, where virtually anything could happen. And Brett and my lives were the awful living proof.

During the final months of the school year, my actual time attending classes was slowly dwindling down to the bare minimum needed to keep me from getting expelled. I was becoming an emotional and physical wreck, covering up the truth with alcohol. Cutting classes and missing lacrosse games became the norm; it wasn't long before I was dropped from the team. Doing homework and studying were things of the past, and what few tests I did show up to take only contributed to the failing grades that were becoming the fourth quarter standard of my final year of school. And if you're wondering how I graduated...I didn't. Not that year. But my report card and incomplete classes were the least contributing factor to that end.

Through it all, unbelievably, incredibly, Angel stuck by my side. Not because she was okay with what I had done and what I was doing, but because she wasn't the kind of person who could ever give up on someone when they were down. Angel really cared for me and knew if she left at this low point in my life, there was a good chance I would never turn myself around. So Angel hung in there with me trying to help me get through, but the fear that she would leave if I got my act together only fed into my self-destructive mental state. The poor girl had no idea what she was in for.

Being in a fraternity was the perfect cover for my obvious cries for help. The anger and frustrations I felt from my situation were just barely under control, but when I was drunk or high, I began to lash out at every chance I got. My Delta brothers loved my aggression...as long as it wasn't aimed at them. But the one person I desperately wanted to vent my hostility on was nowhere to be found. Not surprisingly, Jimmy O left town shortly after he was cleared of the crimes he'd committed and Brett was in prison awaiting trial to take the fall. But he and I would meet again.

* * *

June is an incredible month for all students and especially exciting for those graduating high school. And for Baldwin High seniors, after 12 long years of schooling—13 if you include kindergarten—they were finally moving onto the next exciting stage of their lives. Notice that I said, "they" not "we."

Under normal circumstances, the month would be filled with endless celebrations for the graduating class, the crown jewel being the prom. But for me, these were not normal circumstances. As I was failing all of my classes—and I had not been accepted to any colleges because of it —I was ineligible to graduate and not allowed to attend the prom. If you didn't pass even one class, you were not permitted to go; I was failing eight.

Angel, on the other hand, was acing all of her classes and graduating with honors. She had been accepted into a top undergrad school, her first step toward medical school. The contrast between the two of us was beyond embarrassing. Of course, Angel could attend the prom and bring a date, so I got in by default. I sure showed them.

Being that my girlfriend had worked so hard in school, and the prom was so important to her, despite my depleted mental state, I vowed to do everything in my power to make that night as special for Angel as she hoped it would be. When I was sober, I clearly saw that things were not just about me. But that's the catch.

The pomp, circumstance, and preparation for the big night were enough to make me forget for a moment what a mess my life was and feel almost like a normal high school senior. I had somehow been able to keep my failing grades and ineligibility to graduate from my parents for the time being, so—as false as it might be—I kept up the pretense that everything was A-OK in the world of Bobby Kovac. Going to the prom really sold the lie to my mom and dad.

* * *

In 1973 proms were a big deal, but they had yet to reach the level of insanity the event creates in most communities today. The red carpet and searchlights at the prom entrance with adoring families and friends cheering for each attendee's arrival like they were Hollywood stars had yet to become fashionable. This said, there was plenty of preparation that went into a prom night. Girls wore gowns, "men" rented tuxes, corsages were expected to be pinned on upon arrival at your date's house, and plans needed to be made for an entire evening continuing past the end of the actual prom itself. When the official prom was over, the party would continue, and everyone went out on the town. The cost of this momentous affair could really add up. So in an effort to make the night as perfect as possible, I got it together enough to get some part-time work to raise the cash I would need to pay for it all. I really did love Angel and wanted her to have a great night.

Hard as it is for some to imagine, in the '70s, an easy way for a young man to make some quick cash was to work for a landscaper cutting lawns. Today you won't see any self-respecting high school student doing a job like that; you might think that it's the exclusive domain of people born "south of the border." The mere suggestion that a natural-born citizen of the United States pick up a leaf blower is considered offensive by most teens. Better they turn to their parents for financial support. In some cases, mom and dad will actually pay their own children to do the things around the house that at one time were simply considered chores. But I digress...

Focusing on the big day fast approaching and working hard doing spring cleanups with a local company was having a positive sobering effect on me. It gave me a goal and a purpose. As long as I was working or dealing with the various parts of the coming prom night, I was in a good place. It wasn't until I was alone that thoughts of Brett set in. When I look back on it now, I realize that it was the quiet before the storm. And a hell of a storm was brewing.

CHAPTER TWENTY

The day of the prom finally arrived, and the weather couldn't have been more perfect. As usual, I had been monitoring it all week, and the reports were clear and dry for days before and after. It wouldn't be the weather that ruined the prom.

Prom is a full-day affair, so it's a big win whenever the weather cooperates. In true '70s prom fashion, a bunch of us agreed to share the expense of renting a limo for the big night, adding yet another level of grandeur to the evening. Angel's two girlfriends' dates, Carl, and I all kicked in for a long white stretch with a driver to match. Cheesy by today's standards, but back then we were cruising in style.

Partying is a very traditional part of the prom experience. People who only drink a little, or even some who never drink at all, will indulge and overindulge on prom night. I didn't need an excuse to drink on a normal day, but today I had the world's blessing. Contemporary limousine rentals have over-the-top strict rules about underage drinking. Drivers have lost their jobs and limo companies their licenses over lawsuits involving high school kids drinking in their cars. But back then, the drinking age was 18, not 21, and most of the prom goers were of or close to it. So the "cool" limos came fully stocked with booze.

I really didn't know Angel's friends' dates too well, but Carl and I always got along great and had become even closer after I destroyed my relationship with The Bretts. The two of us were sharing the full-blown prom experience shoulder-to-shoulder. Since the real partying wouldn't start until the limo arrived, in the spirit of the day, we made sure to pick up a six-pack of beer to hold us over until then. We were ready to get our drink on.

First up that morning were haircuts—it was the '70s, so hair styling was more like it—and a beer. Sure it was early, but...prom. Then it was time to get our matching baby blue tuxes—another beer—then we swung by the florist and picked up the corsages we had ordered... followed by a third beer each. By mid-afternoon, we were already approaching "half in the bag" as the saying goes, with completely in the bag not too far off.

The long pre-prom process continued into the mid-afternoon with our limo going from house to house picking up each of the guys, now dressed to the nines, then doing the same for our dates. Of course, every stop required more drinking. By then, we had moved on to the hard stuff stocked in the limo.

At each of the girl's homes came the obligatory parents' presenting of their sacrificial virgin to the male suitor followed by fussing and fawning over the embarrassed couple with an equally awkward photo session for posterity. I'm not saying that all girls attending proms are there to lose their virginity—or some of the boys for that matter—but it's well known that many a young lady does "save herself" for prom night...and the guys are fully aware of it.

All kidding aside, prom really is the first time you get a glimpse of the men and women high school seniors will become. All dressed up with their hair done—and most of them 18 years old or close to it—they are presented as young adults with none of the usual visual trappings of the children they really still are. And without the stigma of the school caste system, you get to see how handsome some of the less popular boys are and how beautiful so many of the unpopular, nerdier girls became while nobody was giving them the time of day. My Angel was living proof of that. Prom is a glimpse through a camera lens to the future. If only I had been able to see mine.

Angel was the last of the girls to be picked up, and by the time we got there, I was feeling no pain but still holding it together. The energy of the day was so positive, and everyone was in such a great mood, it covered most of the sins and stupidity of drunkenness. And to be fair, everybody was drinking. Just not to the extent that I was.

The front yard of the Levitano house was littered with every friend, neighbor, and relative they had—most of them Sauce Sunday and holiday regulars—and when Angel stepped out of that front door held open by her father, she was absolutely stunning. Angel was everything I just said about seeing seniors as adults...times ten. Her hair, her gown, her heels—and the woman under, in, and on them—were incredible. Not only was I speechless...the sight of her was literally sobering. Angel's dad spotted the look of shock and awe on my face.

"You got lucky, son," he said with a smile. "Don't blow it."

"Yes sir," I replied, suddenly nervous.

I silently extended the box holding the purple orchid corsage for which I had raked until I had blisters to afford, and her mom thankfully took it from my shaking hands. She opened it and carefully pinned it on the strap of the plunging neckline of Angel's gown that revealed the woman she had become like nothing she had ever worn before. She was definitely not Flatsy Patsy anymore. There was no way I could have handled that task.

Next came the photos with a throng of onlookers taking the mundane event to the next level; there were so many cameras going off it looked like paparazzi. I couldn't wait to get the hell out of there with Angel and finally let the night begin. But before we could go, there was one last shot to be taken: prom couple and proud parents. Angel's mom stood next to her, and her dad stood by my side. As the cameras again flashed incessantly, I heard a low growl in my ear.

"You smell like a distillery."

It was Angel's dad, still smiling for the cameras and talking through his clenched teeth.

"You better sober the hell up or–"

"I know, I know," I said cutting him off with a chuckle. "We're gonna have a gun problem," I finished his sentence through my own clenched teeth.

I would never have said that if I wasn't drunk.

With that, Vito Levitano completely dropped the facade, turned, and stepped right up to my face.

"You have no idea," he snarled, staring at me with unblinking snake eyes.

There was no missing that comment.

"What's going on?" Angel asked.

"Vito," her mother nervously interjected, "leave Bobby alone."

"Is everything alright, Daddy?"

"Everything is going to be just fine," Angel's father answered, still glaring at me. "Isn't that right, Bobby?"

"Yes, Mr. Levitano," I said, giving the only acceptable answer to the implied threat of that statement.

With that, I sidestepped "the bear" and, taking Angel's hand, led her to the limo. All the family and friends cheered as we headed down the walkway to the car. The only thing missing was rice.

Vito Levitano's threat did have an effect on me...for about a minute. But as the limo had pulled away, I quickly downed a couple more shots of liquid courage, and demon alcohol swept away any memory of Angel's father. The party was on. Well, at least my party was.

During the short ride from Angel's house to Baldwin High School where the prom was being held, things quickly went from bad to worse. With a few more shots, Bobby Kovac was completely gone, and "New Kid" was in full effect...asshole factor on 10.

Let me be clear, this is not who Bobby Kovac was...this is what Bobby Kovac had become. A year of missteps, misfortune, and bad choices had led me to become a person I never thought I'd be...but there I was.

I got loud, I got rowdy, and my frat brother Carl was right there with me. Angel's friends were terrified. The girls were smart kids like Angel, and their dates were, well...smart kids' dates. They would have been a better fit in The Bretts' prom limo than rolling with two Delta brothers. And they couldn't have done anything to stop us if they'd wanted to.

Angel was completely embarrassed by my behavior.

"Bobby, please," she implored, "you're ruining it for everybody."

"Ruining what?" I drunkenly countered. "This is supposed to be a party! School's over, right? We're graduating!"

"You're not."

Out of nowhere, Carl's date, Kathy—a sorority girl who was used to hanging with frat guys—dropped some truth on me, and the car went silent, myself included.

"This isn't even your prom. You're Angel's date," she added.

Then Kathy twisted the knife.

"You shouldn't even be here."

There's nothing more dangerous than an embarrassed drunk. For a couple of seconds, I sat silent, turning red, as shame set in. Then...I completely lost it.

"WHO THE FUCK ARE YOU TO TALK TO ME LIKE THAT, YOU THETA SLUT!?!?"

There are certain lines in civilized company that you're not supposed to cross. That was definitely one of them. Then Carl lost it.

"DON'T TALK TO MY GIRLFRIEND LIKE THAT, NEW KID!"

"WHAT THE HELL ARE YOU GONNA DO ABOUT IT...BLACK KID!?"

And another line was crossed.

Stretch limousines appear to be big on the outside, but they are anything but roomy inside. Still, Carl launched himself at me like we were in a parking lot; the two of us started rolling around in what limited space there was, throwing punches. Horrified and desperate to escape the melee, the other six people in the car somehow crammed together onto the single bench seat meant for two on the opposite end of the car. Then...

"BOBBY KOVAC, IF YOU DON'T STOP RIGHT NOW, MY HAND TO GOD, I WILL NEVER SPEAK TO YOU AGAIN!!!"

Angel had never sounded so Italian. Not only hadn't I heard her scream like that before, but I also knew that was her most solemn oath. She wasn't kidding. I stopped immediately. So did Carl.

"Real classy, Carl," Kathy said, shaking her head.

Brought back to earth but still very drunk, Carl and I went into apologetic bad kids mode.

"We're cool. We're cool," I said, putting an arm around Carl's shoulder and trying to sound like we were actually okay when we most definitely were not.

"Just lettin' off a little steam," Carl added as casually as he could, slipping his arm awkwardly around my shoulder to sell the whole "buddies" thing.

It might have been believable if Carl's nose wasn't bleeding and my lip wasn't dripping blood onto the front of my white tuxedo shirt and baby blue lapels.

Just then the car came to a stop. We had arrived at the school; the driver had pulled up to the front walkway. Outside were dozens of prom attendees talking, checking each other out, and just enjoying the beautiful spring early evening.

The divider that separated the driver from the passengers in the limo suddenly rolled down.

"Nobody puked back dere, did dey?" Tony, our driver, said in his perfect "Lawnguyland" accent.

Then he turned and saw Carl and my condition.

"Shit! Did youse guys bleed on my seats?!"

His accent really was exquisite.

We assured Tony that nobody had done either and started to get out of the clown car. I'm calling it a clown car because watching eight grown men and women wearing gowns, high heels, and tuxedos climb out of a single car door at the back of a stretch limo is something to behold. I don't care what you've seen on TV or at a movie premiere; there's simply no way of doing it gracefully. One after the other, the two male escorts, followed by all four of our dates, struggled to exit with even a modicum of dignity. The six of them just barely pulled it off...then came Carl and me.

Carl stumbled out of the limo and nearly wiped out, but using all four of his limbs, he righted himself at the last second and scrambled to a standing position. This feat garnished an audible, "Whoa!" from the crowd. Then I came out and did a full-face plant. No stumble, no tumble; I just got out of the car and fell right on my face. It almost seemed like I planned it. Living up to her name, Angel rushed over to help me up; I can only imagine the shame she must have felt.

"I got it, I got it," I said indignantly, protesting the assist.

Nothing could have been further from the truth. When I finally did get to my feet, in addition to the bloody lip and stains on my shirt and jacket, I now had a torn knee with a growing bloodstain on my pants. It was a matched set. I looked over and saw that Angel now had my blood on her beautiful gown. Shit.

When we finally got inside, the prom was already in full swing. The theme that year was "Under the Sea," a tribute to the waters surrounding Long Island—predating the song from the Disney film *The Little Mermaid* by at least 15 years—and the gym was heavily decorated in shades of green and blue to give the feeling of being...well, you know. You could barely tell people were celebrating their coming graduation in a gymnasium.

Baldwin High favorites Dusk was on stage playing a cover of Alice Cooper's "Schools Out," a hit from the previous year that was sure to become a perennial end-of-school-year favorite. Twenty-five years later it is still played incessantly every June on the radio. Dusk was comprised of five longhairs that by day sat with the other freaks along the window next to Delta and Omega in the Commons. The band was pretty good, the standout being the group's lead singer; some choir geek with a really good voice. He actually went on to become pretty famous. Dusk had everyone up, dancing and singing along.

Carl, Kathy, Angel, and I weren't halfway across the dance floor when our frat brothers rushed us and proceeded to pull Carl and me away. This really was their M.O. New Kid's reputation as a "partier" had grown over the last couple of months. Flasks and small bottles of various school contraband were shoved in my face to be imbibed, and I obliged.

Dusk rocked on, and the celebration was in full effect.

CHAPTER TWENTY-ONE

W aking up in a jail cell is an experience that's tough to describe. Especially when you don't remember being arrested in the first place. You open your eyes and think for the briefest second that you're in your own bed, then the truth comes rushing in. Cinderblock walls, bars, a sink, and a toilet in the room! This was my first time being incarcerated, but I had no doubt about where I was. Then I started to feel my body.

I wasn't new to the symptoms of a hangover—my head pounded, my mouth was Sahara dry, and everything was way too bright and loud. Body-aches are a normal part of the experience, too, but this time there was more. I could definitely tell that my jaw was swollen; it was difficult to open my mouth. I'd clearly been in a fight, and my bruised knuckles told me that I had probably given as good as I got, maybe better. Then there was a sudden loud banging on the cell bars. It sounded like it was directly on my skull.

"Rise and shine, Princess," a too-loud, too-authoritative voice boomed.

This was clearly a practiced wake-up meant to establish authority. It worked. I sat up as best I could and looked toward the voice. A cop stood outside the cell staring at me like I was some science experiment.

"Where am I?" I heard my voice say somewhere in the cloudy distance.

"Seriously?" the officer responded, not realizing it was just a poorly-phrased rhetorical question. "You're in jail, idiot."

Now he sounded like my dad. Oh shit, my dad!

"What for?" I heard myself ask.

"You really don't remember?" he asked in disbelief.

Now who was asking a stupid question? I couldn't believe he had never dealt with someone who had been blackout drunk before. Well, now he had.

"So what did I do?"

"The big one? Felony assault," he answered, sounding a little happy about it.

Damn! I knew that was as serious as it sounded.

"Who did I hit?'

"How the fuck should I know? I wasn't the arresting officer," he answered, now sounding more than a little happy. "Wanna know the best part? You're 18, asshole. You'll be tried as an adult. I'm so tired of you hoodlums getting off because you're minors."

Hoodlums? The guy sounded like a cop caricature from the '50s. If any part of me was pretending it didn't know this situation was next level, it did now.

"Get the hell on your feet," the cop barked at me. "You made bail."

To say the ride home with my parents was uncomfortable would be the understatement of all time. My father couldn't even find words to express the anger he felt toward me, but the raw disgust came off him in waves. My mother, on the other hand, took full blame for my fall from grace; her disappointment and hurt were palpable.

"This is all my fault. I wasn't there when you needed me," she said, crying. "I just didn't give you enough love."

The only thing she left out was not breastfeeding me long enough. How could I possibly respond to that? It's not you, Mom, it's me? Talk about ringing hollow. She came as close to self-flagellation as a person could without actually breaking out a whip and beating herself. It was heartbreaking for me to watch and listen to.

Putting the pieces of my lost night together wasn't very difficult but did require a number of phone calls and conversations with people who were there. The one person I didn't call was Angel.

The story goes that the drunker the frat guys at the prom got, the rowdier and more violent we became. The most innocent bump on the dance floor turned into a confrontation, drunken brawls were erupt-ing...and New Kid was doing his thing. Of course, there were teachers on duty serving as chaperones, but when dealing with drunk, stoned, fully-developed seniors, there's only so much they could actually do.

That's when the reinforcements were called in, namely...the Physical Education Department.

Now, not only are most gym teachers capable of getting physical—they were once dumb, rowdy jocks, too—but no one knew our M.O. better than the coaches. And while they were usually pretty cool and a little too understanding about our hijinks, you could only push them so far. Unlike regular teachers who withered from aggressive students, gym teachers seemed to love it when some kid got in their face. And when one did—or in this case more than one—they transformed back to the high school/college assholes they once were and went into full hard-on mode.

Things finally spiraled completely out of control. Food and drinks started to be thrown, tables were flipped, and chairs were hurled; and the physical education department, along with ex-Marine shop teacher Mr. Medlock—who all seemed to be waiting in the wings for just such a moment—poured out onto the dance floor and started to manhandle the culprits. This was the '70s when teachers could not only get away with stuff like that but were often applauded for their actions. Now here's where the felony assault charge came in.

Apparently, I was minding my own business, dancing and having a good time—read: running around, knocking people over, throwing food, and flipping tables—when Mr. Medlock suddenly came up behind me and tried to put me in a chokehold. I told you before that I had some training, well that was a bit of an understatement. When we lived on the base in Dayton, I took Jiu-Jitsu from the time I was seven until we moved, and I was the state champ in my first year of high school. The point was, I had enough training to react instinctively to a dangerous situation, and when he wrapped his big arm around my neck and started to bring his other arm over my shoulder to lock in the hold, I tucked my chin, grabbed his arm with both hands, flipped him over my back and onto the floor in one swift move. This was pure instinct; a chokehold can literally kill you. But those facts didn't seem to matter because Mr. Medlock landed on his head and broke his neck. Fortunately, he wasn't paralyzed, but that didn't seem to matter. I was then jumped and held by three coaches while Coach Landers the lacrosse and football coach—the same one who earlier that year had told me I was Baldwin Varsity Material—punched me in the face and knocked me out cold.

The police came, and ambulances were called; even the fire department showed up for some reason. The teachers and prom staff tried to salvage something out of the ruined prom, but once the music was shut down and the lights turned on, the magic was gone. No one believed they were "under the sea" anymore. The Baldwin High School, Class of '73 Senior Prom had been ruined. That would be the headline; that would be the memory. And I was to blame.

I didn't try to see or call Angel for days. Having pieced together the whole story, I could easily fill in the blanks of what she went through that night. I'd heard enough about what happened to her from some of her friends.

Apparently, she didn't just let me do my thing. Angel did everything she could to stop me. Not just for my well-being, but for everyone at the prom. She could tell where the evening was headed and tried to intervene, to get in the way of the self-destructive force that was New Kid. She fought her way through the throng of rowdy DZO members to literally pull the alcohol out of my hands, but I just grabbed more and kept drinking. Angel then tried to pull me aside and calm me down, but I shook her off and went back to my cronies. And when I got in my first fight of the night, she stepped in between my nameless opponent and me, only to have me knock her to the floor in a drunken rage. To be clear, I never hit her, but I might as well have. My complete disregard for how hard she was trying to help probably hurt her more than being shoved out of the way. By the time the riot broke out, Angel had long given up on the prom, on the night...and on me. And I was too drunk to even notice.

But I was sober now. And after three days of avoiding her, I manned up enough to face the music and at least give her the decency of telling me off.

I wouldn't dare go to her house. I was sure that her father was going to make good on his longstanding threat. I didn't know if it was a gun or a bat problem, but I knew that I had broken my promise to him and had definitely hurt his daughter. Maybe not physically, but I had broken her heart; that counts. So I went to the school to find her; I hadn't been there since the prom. There was no sense pretending I was still a graduating student anymore. My parents knew everything, and I was out on bail; graduating from high school wasn't even a consideration. I had bigger problems to worry about.

I pulled my car over at end of High School Drive by the student-parking area. The name of the road has since been changed to Ethel Kloberg Lane in memory of that sturdy Baldwin High dean of students with the strange name, but it's still the same east/west cut-through that went from Brookside Avenue to Grand Avenue. It gave me a birds-eye view of everyone who came and went from the front exit of the school. I wasn't worried about missing her. Angel would never walk across the sports field on the other side of the building; she lived in the opposite direction.

As I sat waiting, I listened to Led Zeppelin's "Thank You" on an endless loop, the lyrics and Robert Plant's tortured voice alternately giving me hope and breaking my heart at the same time. A song about everlasting love and the pain of losing it, this was the soundtrack to my Angel vigil until I finally saw her walk out of the building. I didn't know whether to race up to her in my car, exposing my passion, or roll up slowly and try to play it cool. I opted to get out of my car and go it on foot, hoping against hope that she would at least talk to me and making it more difficult for her to just walk away. But she didn't.

"What's going on, New Kid," she said, cutting me to the quick. She never called me that; I was always her Bobby.

"Don't call me that," I said, trying not to sound as hurt as I was.

"Why not? As far as I can see, Bobby Kovac is gone."

Now she turned and started walking away. I followed her in what I hoped was nonthreatening pursuit.

"No, Angel, he's still here," I countered. "He was lost, but he's finally snapped out of it."

I don't know why I was talking about myself in the third person.

"Oh really?" she said. "What did it take, destroying the prom or being arrested for assault?"

"Neither," I said. "It was breaking your and my mom's hearts."

Angel said nothing in response but stopped walking and looked at me. Then...

"Bobby..."

Hope.

"You've destroyed your life. I can't let you destroy mine, too."

"It's not destroyed," I said, not knowing who the hell I was kidding. "I can fix it."

"Fix it?" Angel said in complete disbelief. "You failed high school— you're not graduating—there's no college in your future, and you broke the gym teacher's neck! This isn't a car you can repair! You're going to be tried on charges of felony assault!"

"My lawyer thinks I'll get off with probation–"

"BOBBY!" Angel shouted. "Probation? That's your best answer?"

I didn't know what to say. She started to cry.

"Tell me you're going to change. Tell me you're going to finish school. Tell me you're going to get your life back—our life back! But for the love of God, don't tell me you're hanging our dreams on getting probation!"

Men crying used to be taboo, but times have changed. These days it's considered acceptable for boys and men to openly show their less masculine emotions. See that? Even that statement is limiting and stigmatizing. It implies that crying is a specifically feminine response. It's not. And these days there are a lot of people who feel the idea of males not being allowed to show such a basic emotion is oppressive and draconian. "Big boys don't cry" was literally an accepted child-rearing mantra for centuries. Women cry, men don't. But these days, boys and men are encouraged to express their full range of feelings, including crying. It's now common to see grown men crying their eyes out in movies, television shows, and even real-life moments broadcast on the news. But that's not how I was raised.

As a kid, I was what used to be known as a "crybaby." A label that virtually doesn't exist today—but oddly is still in the dictionary—a crybaby was a boy who wept at the drop of a hat. If he was hurt, scared, lonely, hungry, sad, or whatever, the crybaby would openly take this action as a way to show his feelings. Of course, this was completely unacceptable in the '50s and '60s, especially for the son of a military man. So my father—and mother for that matter—worked on curing me of my embarrassing habit. Sometimes it was as simple as a smack in the head with a "Stop crying you big baby!" to drive the point home, while other times—most of the time, for that matter— humiliation was used as a teaching tool. It was not uncommon for my father to openly laugh, mock, ridicule, or imitate me when I started crying, thus embarrassing and shaming me into stopping. As a child, I remember there was a tune my mother used to play on the piano and sing that would bring me to tears every time. It was an old Woody

Guthrie folk song called "So Long It's Been Good to Know You" about saying goodbye forever to friends, family, and lovers; and for some reason, it triggered deep sadness in me. Every time I heard it, I would start to cry. Sweet kid, right? Well, not by early '60s standards. When I got to eight or nine years old, my father decided that it wasn't cute anymore, and my mother played the song over and over while they sang and laughed at me as I cried. I begged them to stop, but they wouldn't. Eventually, I learned never to cry.

But I did now. For the first time since I was nine years old, I cried. I cried and cried. For Brett, for Angel, for my mom, and for myself, I let all the pain go at once.

"Angel, I'm sorry, I'm sorry, I'm sorry, I'm so sorry!" I gushed as the floodgates opened. "I got lost. I'm lost. I just tried to help my friend, and everything went wrong!"

All of the raw emotions that I'd been holding in, burying with drugs, booze, fighting, and partying came pouring out, the full realization of how one brief moment in time had changed everything in my life forever.

"I hurt everybody I love, and now I just want something—anything—to be right," I sobbed, suddenly aware that Angel was holding me.

"Something can be right. We can be right," she said comforting me.

"How?" I blubbered.

"By starting over," Angel answered. "We go back to before you helped Brett, to before you joined the fraternity, to that first day in the cafeteria when you saw me and I saw you. Just us. Bobby and Angel."

The only thing I could think to say was the title of the Zeppelin song I had just been listening to.

"Thank you."

"NEW KID!"

A panicked voice desperately interrupted our healing moment.

"IT'S GAMMA NU!" the voice continued.

I turned to see Mofo Creeder half hanging out of his car window, shouting to me.

"You gotta help! They attacked us at Burger King, and there's a shit-load of them!"

This was a turning point, and I wasn't about to make the wrong choice again.

"Sorry, Mofo…," I started to say when…

"JIMMY O IS THERE!" he shouted.

This stopped me in my tracks for a brief second, but I had already lost so much; I had to let it go.

"Mofo, I can't–"

"HE STABBED CARL!" Mofo finished with the words he should have started with.

Now I couldn't walk away. Jimmy O wouldn't stop just because I didn't respond to his aggression. And I couldn't let him hurt another one of my friends just to get at me. I turned to Angel…she saw the look on my face.

"Bobby," she pleaded, "please…don't…."

"But Angel," I said, desperately, "First Brett and now Carl? Somebody's got to stop this guy."

"But why does it have to be you?" she implored.

"Because it's got to be somebody…," I answered softly.

Tears were running down Angel's cheeks. She dropped her head and shook it slowly. Still, I turned and ran for Creeder's car.

"Don't worry," I shouted to her as I jumped in, "I'll be right back!"

I lied to her again.

CHAPTER TWENTY-TWO

Burger King had been a frat boy hangout since it opened in the late '60s. Located on Grand Avenue just north of Sunrise Highway and the Long Island Railroad train trestle, it was pretty perfectly situated. Geographically, it sat between North and South Baldwin, on the downside, it was close to Freeport, Rockville Centre, and relatively close to Oceanside, homes of rival high school sports teams...and fraternities. That made it the perfect spot for hostile interaction. If you wanted to get into a fight with another school or frat on your home turf, Grand Avenue Burger King was the place to go.

When Marky and I got there, we were on the west side of Grand Avenue heading south. BK was on the east side of the road, so we were directly across the street. The scene in the parking lot was like something out of a movie; it was a war zone. A quick assessment said there had to have been more than 50 members of Black and White fighting an amalgam of Baldwin fraternities who just happened to be there and had banded together to make a stand against a superior force. And what a force it was. I told you how members of Gamma Nu rarely graduated, went to college, or left town. Delta Gamma Nu, having been around for a number of years by then, meant there were semi-active members now well into their 20s...and it looked like their entire alumnus was in the Burger King parking lot.

I told you fights like these were usually scheduled events. Once again, Gamma Nu had broken the rules. And this wasn't a fair fight either; it was the ugliest of street brawls with every kind of weapon besides a gun—as far as I could see—being used against Baldwin guys who didn't fight dirty. But Black and White did, and our side was clearly overwhelmed and losing; they badly needed help.

Creeder didn't pull over so we would have to cross the street to join the action. Without stopping, he made a wide U-turn going from the extreme right lane southbound, cutting through and across four lanes of traffic, and swinging right in front of the parking lot. It was dramatic, it was dangerous, and a bunch of cars just barely missed hitting us, but it was the exact move called for given the situation.

As he was making his move and we crossed to the other side of the road, I spotted Carl. He was on the ground propped up against the wall of the fast-food restaurant, his t-shirt soaked with blood. Mr. Reichman, the manager of Burger King—who had seen a lot of fights, but nothing as insane as this—was kneeling down beside him pressing what looked like a red rag against Carl's wound; when we got closer, I could see it was red with Carl's blood.

I was already throwing the door open as Mofo screeched to a halt.

"Get Carl to the nearest hospital now!" I shouted to Creeder as I jumped out of the still-moving car, the forward motion and sudden stop literally launching me into the thick of things.

I ran into the parking lot and started pulling Black and White off my guys; my guys being anybody who was fighting a member of Gamma Nu. I was in a berserker rage and took every bit of anger and frustration from my life's situation out on each one of them, with only one true target in mind...Jimmy O.

Much like the gunfights of the Old West, street fights in movies and on TV are always romanticized, choreographed dances where each combatant gives and gets, never seeming to show the real effects of the blow that was delivered or received. One guy gets hit, stumbles back, shakes it off, then charges forward and gives his opponent pretty much the same. That's tit-for-tat fantasy bullshit, not street-fight reality. In actual street fighting, there's a lot more pushing and shoving with wild punches being thrown, rarely hitting their mark. Add to that a whole lot of grappling—not the "Gracie Family" MMA kind, the desperately holding on kind—and you've got the truth of the average brawl. But this wasn't a fight...this was retribution. Retribution for what, I'm not exactly sure. Maybe it was for the years of imagined oppression Gamma Nu had suffered at the hands of DZO, or maybe it was just for the terrible life most of those Black and White miscreants had been dealt. But Delta Gamma Nu had a giant chip on its collective shoulder, and this was the moment they decided to make somebody pay. Unfortunately for them, I had my own emotional issues, which I was happy to unload on each and every one of them.

My plan was simple: help out as many of my friends and brothers as possible—while not getting bogged down fighting anyone in particular —as I searched for my nemesis; the man responsible for Brett being in jail, stabbing Carl, ruining my life, and causing me so much pain...Jimmy Fucking O.

As I ran from fight to fight pulling, kicking, punching, shoulder flipping, and leg sweeping my way through the parking lot, I asked everyone the same question...

"Where is he?"

I didn't have to specify whom. Everyone knew exactly whom I was looking for, and while they all knew Jimmy O was there, no one could say exactly where. All I got was a bunch of general direction stuff:

"Over there!"

"By the dumpsters!"

"In the back!"

Nothing was consistent or really useful, but still, I fought on.

Across the parking lot, I saw Tank up against a car in a losing battle with two bruisers from Black and White. These guys looked like they were in their 40s. Not only were they double-teaming him, but one had a Billy club, and the other was wearing a pair of brass knuckles. Brass knuckles! I ran up behind Tank's two adversaries, yanked the one with the brass knuckles back, and threw him to the ground. Then I pulled the club out of the hand of the other one and cracked him across the face with it. Quid pro quo. Tank was a bit dazed and holding his head. I could see bumps already rising where he had been hit and punched.

"Tank, have you seen Jimmy O?" I repeated the same question like it was my mantra.

Tank lifted his head to answer me...and then his eyes went wide.

"What is it?" I asked.

He took his hand off his head and pointed.

I spun around in the direction of his "arrow" just in time to see Jimmy O right behind me, with a murderous look in his eyes, bearing down as he took a full swing at my face and head with a baseball bat. He was "going for the fence."

EPILOGUE

P resent day.

I stopped talking and let the punch line of my story set in. Punch line may seem like an incredibly callous word for all that happened, but after all these years I have come to view it as God's cruel joke. And it was somehow appropriate. I thought telling my story might, after all these years, free me of the darkness. It did not.

All four of my fellow carpoolers sat in stunned silence. I guess they never expected a story like that to come out of average guy Robert Kovac's mouth. Well, they shouldn't judge a book by its cover. Just because someone appears to be normal—whatever that is—doesn't mean they don't have a story or two to tell.

I couldn't believe rush hour traffic had lasted long enough for me to tell my entire story in one sitting. Rush hour my ass. Now we were stuck in crosstown traffic. It's the worst. Pure aggravation every time you come to another stupid reason you're going nowhere fast. A lot like life, I guess.

"So what happened to you?" James asked, finally breaking the silence.

"What the hell do you think happened, James?" Tom replied, genuinely irritated. "Look at the scar on his head!"

"Whatever you're all imagining," I said, "it was much worse."

"Worse like…" Marie trailed off.

"Worse like they performed last rites on me," I finished Marie's sentence for her.

"You died?" Alex asked in disbelief.

"Yup…twice," I said, way too flippantly. "Jimmy O caved in my head and bruised my brain. They had to remove a section of my skull to release the pressure and keep me from becoming a complete vegetable. What I've got up there now," I said, pointing to the top of my head, "is a metal plate."

"So you're only an incomplete vegetable?" James quipped in a piss-poor attempt to relieve the tension by joking.

"Holy shit, James," Marie said, "that was awful."

I don't think I've ever heard Marie curse.

"Really, dude," added Tom, "get a grip."

"Sorry, Robert," James said sheepishly.

"It's okay," I replied, letting him off the hook. "A part of me still feels I deserved every single thing I got."

"So what happened?" Tom pushed, looking for more of an answer.

"The only way they saved me was by inducing a coma; I was uncon-scious for six months. They had no idea what I would be like when they finally brought me out."

More silence.

Gratefully, my mind wandered back to the bumper-to-bumper traffic at hand. Robert Moses had a plan to erect multiple sky bridges from the east side to the west side over the city. Shame it never happened.

"And Jimmy O?" Alex asked, interrupting the quiet and pulling me back in.

"Jimmy O?" I repeated, letting out an odd chortle. "His lawyers got him off with a slap on the wrist."

"What?" Tom said in disbelief.

"Oh, yeah," I continued, still stunned myself all these years later. "They used a 'crime of passion,' 'heat of the moment' defense."

"That figures," Marie said in disgust.

"My lawyers couldn't prove that Jimmy O was out to get me, and it was undeniable that I was looking for him so..."

I drifted off.

"So...where is he now?" James asked, popping the million-dollar question.

I paused, not for dramatic effect, but because the answer still haunted me.

"The next year, Jimmy O was arrested for abducting, raping, and torturing a mother of two in his neighborhood," I answered, pausing again. "Then he burned her alive."

Jaws definitely dropped on that one. I wondered if their thoughts were rushing back to that afternoon tea with my mother like mine were. Back then I didn't think something like that was even a possibility.

"He's doing a life sentence with no chance of parole," I finished. Justice finally served.

This shit was so beyond comprehension that it completely shut down the conversation. What can you say after something like that? It was Tom who broke the silence this time.

"So you never saw Brett again...did you?" he asked with the answer he was expecting clearly implied in the question.

"The second I opened my eyes from the coma," I answered, stunning the car.

"What?" James said, not believing his ears.

"Do you mean like in a vision or a dream?" Maria suggested.

"Nope; I mean like for real," I replied.

"He came to the hospital to see you?" Alex followed.

"I told you that I couldn't be at his trial," I started, "now you know why. Brett heard what had happened to me before he got out. The fact was we were both victims of Jimmy O—each of us nearly getting a life sentence—that softened his anger and hatred toward me. Brett came to see me in the hospital every day of my coma after he was released."

"So the two of you are best friends again?" James asked hopefully.

"No. What we went through changed both of us forever," I began. "How could it not? We would never be high school best buddies, 'Bobby and Brett' again...but we are friends."

We rode in semi-comfortable silence the rest of the way to the parking garage near where we worked. No doubt the coda on the Brett saga was bittersweet. I pulled in and as we were about to get out of the car...

"Wait a second," Marie suddenly said. "Your wife's name is 'Ang.' Is that...?"

"Yeah," I said and smiled.

The End.

ACKNOWLEDGMENTS

Dee Snider would like to thank Ron "I'll get you a book deal!" Starrantino, Stephanie "Da' Publisha'" Larkin and JK Larkin, Ralph Asbury, Don Fury and Ray (O.G. "The Brets"), Roger and Scott Offner (Alpha Sigma Phi), Frederick M. Gross, his book *Fraternal Brotherhood* (Alpha Omega Theta), Baldwin, Long Island, Ardmore Rd., Baldwin Senior High School, Ethel Kloberg (RIP), The Dukes, Dusk, and the early '70s Nassau County South Shore fraternity scene for making my high school years so "lively."

Special thanks to my "Trusted Readers": Bob Snider, Jesse Blaze Snider, Shane Royal Snider, Cody Blue Snider, Mark "Creeder" Snider, Phil Carson, Joe Gerber, Greg Praetorius, Pam Edwards, Ellen Lee, Marty Callner, Malak Akkad, Dan Stanton, Michael Alden, David Katz, John Yonover, Scooter Pietsch, and Ron Starr.

EXTRA SPECIAL THANKS TO JOE "DRUMMER" STEFKO!

ABOUT THE AUTHOR

While perhaps best known as the lead singer of 80's sensation, Twisted Sister, there is so much more to Dee Snider. His hit song-writing credits extend to many genres of music and have been covered by major artists the world over. Celine Dion's version of the Snider penned "Magic of Christmas Day (God Bless Us Everyone) was a significant part of her international, multi-platinum "These Are Special Times" album, the biggest selling holiday album in history.

Dee has starred in *too many* reality TV shows including appearances on three seasons of *Celebrity Apprentice; Gone Country* with John Rich; MTV's *Rock the Cradle* with his son Jesse Blaze; *Growing Up Twisted,* an A&E series featuring the entire Snider family; ABC's *Celebrity Wife Swap,* and most recently FOX's *Masked Singer.* Dee has also been a frequent host on the MTV Networks and, with more than 30 years on the air in terrestrial and satellite radio, has his own, long running, nationally syndicated radio show *House Of Hair* [houseofhaironline.com] which can be heard on more than 250 stations in North America. His voiceover career has resulted in Dee being heard on a multitude of radio and TV commercials, animated shows, documentaries, video games, and even a stint as the voice of MSNBC. Snider is currently the narrator of the hit Reelz Network series, "Breaking the Band".

In 2010, Dee starred on Broadway as *Dennis Dupree* in the Tony award winning musical *Rock Of Ages* and since then his theatre connection has grown. He recorded the critically acclaimed album "Dee Does Broadway" (featuring Patti LuPone and Bebe Neuwirth), and wrote the lyrics, music and book for "A Rock 'n' Roll Christmas Tale" which completed highly successful runs throughout the 2014 (Chicago) and 2015 (Toronto) holiday seasons.

Never setting limits, Dee Snider has co-created "Monsters Rock", a new children's animated series for *Peacock,* released his first fiction novel *"Frats",* and this year will make his directorial debut with his most recent scary screenplay *My Enemy's Enemy.*

So, what's next? *Ask Dee.*